"Your bag is not the designer number I'd expected, Miranda," said Greg. "What's the story there?"

The pastor looked so genuinely interested in her answer that she had to tell him the whole story. "Winnie made it for me about twenty years ago."

"It looks like a well-used treasure," Greg pointed out, endearing himself to her for good. He could have noted instead that the pink corduroy was faded and thin in spots and that it was worn down past the wale from years of use. Instead he'd noticed how cherished it was.

"You're right. It is the one link I have with my mother that I can carry around every day." She fingered the cloth lovingly. "When I was ten, my mother and father had a terrible fight and she left home. The next morning, Father told us that she had been in a terrible accident after she left and had died. Of course we know now that wasn't true...."

* * *

THE SECRETS OF STONELEY: Six sisters face murder, mayhem and mystery .... past.

FA............................ 2007
LITTL........................ y 2007
E........................... 07
THE S....................... l 2007
DE........................... 07
WHE............ ....CK (LIS#56) June 2007

Books by Lynn Bulock

Love Inspired Suspense

Where Truth Lies #56

Love Inspired

Gifts of Grace #80
Looking for Miracles #97
Walls of Jericho #125
The Prodigal's Return #144
Change of the Heart #181
The Harbor of His Arms #204
Protecting Holly #279

Steeple Hill Single Title

Love the Sinner
Less Than Frank

LYNN BULOCK

has been writing since fourth grade and has been a published author in various fields for over twenty years. Her first romantic novel came out in 1989 and has been followed by more than twenty books since then. She lives near Los Angeles, California, with her husband. They have two grown sons.

LYNN BULOCK
Where Truth Lies

Steeple
Hill®

Published by Steeple Hill Books™

Special thanks and acknowledgment are given to
Lynn Bulock for her contribution to
THE SECRETS OF STONELEY miniseries.

STEEPLE HILL BOOKS

Steeple
Hill®

ISBN-13: 978-0-373-44246-1
ISBN-10:   0-373-44246-7

WHERE TRUTH LIES

www.SteepleHill.com

Printed in U.S.A.

Jesus looked at them and said,
"With people it is impossible, but not with God;
all things are possible with God."
—*Mark* 10:27

To Joe, always

And to Toni…she knows why

ONE

Journal entry
June 1

Why is everyone being so horrible to my darling Ronald? How can the police believe that someone with his wealth and reputation might be guilty of murder? If I went to them and confessed, he would be free, but then all my efforts would be in vain. I've worked so hard so that we can be together. Even that awful woman didn't get in our way. Now if his daughters will just stop their infernal digging into the past, maybe Ronald and I can finally be happy.

*W*as her father truly guilty of murder? The question whirled through Miranda Blanchard's thoughts as she tried to concentrate on the familiar, repetitive work of making endpapers for her latest edition of handmade poetry books. Swirling the heavy paper through the color bath to create the marbled design she favored usually took her mind off her troubles. But on this beautiful late-spring day her worries crowded in so close that not even this task succeeded in distracting her.

Setting the latest sheet with its rich green, teal and indigo design aside to dry, Miranda pressed the back of one hand to her throbbing temple. Even gloved and swathed in an apron, with her dark hair swept away from her face, she would probably find a way to dot herself with paint.

Normally her workroom and studio tucked up under the eaves of her family's huge house, near her grandfather Howard's third-floor suite, was a peaceful haven. Cool and pleasant, with pearl-gray walls and a large window to let in just enough light, it was where Miranda went to relax, write poetry and craft the chapbooks and limited editions she made for her own work and a select few other writers.

Relax, or hide? a cynical voice from inside taunted her. Pushing back a stray lock of wavy hair, she could feel the flutter in her stomach and the tightening of her chest that heralded the beginning of a panic attack. Not another one. She couldn't afford one now, when she was so behind in her projects.

She hadn't written anything new in months, or nothing worth keeping, anyway. Even the piece she'd tried to do for her mother's funeral came out flat. Of course when they discovered later that it wasn't Trudy the family had buried, Miranda tried to convince herself that somehow she'd known all along, but she couldn't manage to fool herself that way.

This batch of a hundred books for another poet at the university in Augusta should have been finished weeks ago. So many other things had claimed her attention in the first five months of the year that Miranda had trouble believing everything that had gone on.

From the moment Bianca had produced that picture of Mama with her friend on Cape Cod, dated after her supposed death, life had been a jumble of highs and lows. Trudy Blanchard was apparently alive after all, or at least she had been recently. This last blow had been the most wrenching. Miranda still had flashbacks of her father and sisters around the grave in Stoneley's windswept cemetery, all of them weeping to think that they'd come so close to rediscovering the wife and mother taken from them so long ago, only to find her dead in the house instead.

"You could at least be grateful for what happened," she chided herself out loud, her soft words echoing off the angled ceiling of her studio. Finding grandparents they thought were dead, and learning that Aunt Genie—not her mother—died should have made her ecstatic. Instead, Miranda was caught up in the anxiety around her as her father was arrested for the murder of his sister-in-law.

"He has to be innocent," Miranda said, hoping

the words spoken out loud would calm her nerves and convince her that the statement was true. That was the hard part. Ronald Blanchard might be innocent of Genie's death, but the revelations of the past few months had shown he was far from innocent regarding the faked death and disappearance of his wife, and Miranda couldn't imagine how she and her sisters could ever forgive him for what he'd stolen from them.

Maybe some of her sisters would be able to forgive him. Not her, and probably not Juliet, either, because of the revelation that Ronald had known even before Juliet was born that he wasn't her biological father. Never did he tell any of them. All these years he'd been distant and cold with all his daughters.

Miranda looked down at the paper she should have been swishing through the paint floating on top of the water bath. Instead she'd let this sheet stay there so long while she wrestled with her thoughts that the heavy paper threatened to dissolve back into pulp. "So much for trying to do anything useful today," she muttered.

Three stories below her open window, someone was working in the rose garden. Since she could also make out the drone of a lawn mower, it had to be Aunt Winnie and not one of the gardeners. It only took fifteen minutes for Miranda to clean up her supplies, strip off the gloves and apron and go out to the garden with two tall glasses of lemonade.

"I brought you something to drink," she called to Winnie, glad to see that her aunt had remembered the broad-brimmed straw hat Miranda had got her for Mother's Day just for occasions like this. Winnie never put on sunscreen even though she had the pale complexion that naturally went with her red hair.

That faded red hair threatened to escape its orderly chignon, and Winnie pushed a stray lock away from her face. "Lovely. Put it on the little table there between the chairs and sit down in one of them, Miranda. Keep me company while I tidy things up here. You could use a rest. You've been working too hard as it is."

Over her shoulder, Winnie gave Miranda a pointed look over her shoulder before going back to trimming unkempt spots in one of her pink climbing rosebushes. Miranda knew that what her aunt really wanted to say was that she'd been worrying too much and had too much stress in her life lately. After all, what she did could hardly be called working. While all of her sisters worked, Miranda knew that only someone who loved her as much as Winnie did would call writing poetry and creating handmade books "work."

Even Winnie herself worked outside the house as hard as any two people Miranda knew. The Blanchard fortune allowed her to volunteer her time at the hospital, several related charities and her church. It was a kindness that Winnie could tell her that she was the one working too hard. Still, she took the hint and sank into one of the blue Adirondack chairs, grateful to sit here in the sunshine with the scent of roses and fresh-cut grass around her.

This garden was one of her favorite outdoor places, especially when Winnie was there. Her aunt seemed happy, humming tunelessly and working among her beloved roses. "I'm starting to cull blossoms for the petals I want to dry for Portia's wedding. Won't it be lovely to have them scattered on the runner up the aisle before the bridesmaids and the bride?"

Miranda's throat tightened just thinking about her sister's eventual wedding. Often these days the thought of going anywhere farther than the ornate iron gates at the front of the Blanchard estate made her insides flutter like they did right now. Actually making a move to venture out left her unable to cope.

Adding to her anxiety was Miranda's worry that a Blanchard wedding at Unity Christian Church was guaranteed to become a very public event. The sunlight that felt so welcoming a few minutes before now made beads of perspiration break out on her forehead, and she could feel her breathing become shallow and rapid. This was silly. If she could get here to the rose garden and enjoy the day, why couldn't the thought of a happy event like her sister's wedding be enjoyable as well?

Because you know the media will turn it into

a three-ring circus, that same taunting voice in her head prodded. "Trudy's" funeral had been awful enough. A wedding would only provide more fodder for the gaggle of tabloid reporters who were having a field day at her family's expense.

"Miranda? I'm so sorry, dear. I didn't mean to upset you." Miranda nearly jumped out of her chair at the sound of Winnie's voice, her gloved hand lightly touching her shoulder. "Really, we don't need to worry about that yet. There will be plenty of time to plan the wedding and by the time it rolls around things will probably be so much better." Her aunt's hazel eyes reflected kindness almost to the point of pity as she tried her hardest to calm Miranda down. Taking a deep breath, Miranda willed herself to push away the thoughts making her tense.

"I'm sure you're right, Aunt Winnie." The words came out softly, but at least her voice didn't break.

Even as she spoke, so many questions crowded in. Would there ever be enough time to make things better? Perhaps her father would get out on bail soon, but then what? And how long could Miranda keep holding herself together while she struggled to provide all the support her sisters needed? Although with every passing day they appeared to need her less. Each of them had found a way to move on in life while Miranda stayed here, as tied to the house as her aunt's trellised roses were fastened to their supports.

"What would you think of a little practice run?"

Winnie's eyes shone. "I'm going to a lovely wedding at the church tomorrow and you could come with me."

Miranda shrank back in her chair. "I don't know about that."

"Don't dismiss it out of hand, Miranda," Winnie said. "The couple is just delightful, but no one you know particularly well. We could sit near the back and stay just as long as you felt comfortable. And it would give you a chance to really meet our new minister."

"I'll think about it," Miranda promised her aunt. "How early tomorrow morning do you need to know if I'm going?"

Winnie waved a garden-gloved hand. "It's a one-o'clock wedding, so you can hold off until eleven if you need to. It would do you good to get out and enjoy yourself."

Miranda knew she was right. If only getting out was enjoyable for her. So many possibilities would open up if she could overcome her anxiety about leaving home. She could see her thoughts mirrored in Winnie's eyes. "I'll say even more prayers tonight at bedtime than I usually do for you, Miranda. For strength and courage and peace. Especially for peace."

"Thank you, Aunt Winnie." Miranda got up quickly, walking toward the house before her aunt could see how deeply those words had affected her. Going up the back stairs toward her studio again,

Miranda climbed an entire flight before she realized she was humming the song.

Perhaps prayer gave Winnie peace, but Miranda's fragile peace was bound up in this song. It had been a part of her forever, the haunting melody soothing her through the worst of times.

During her recent visit, her grandmother Eleanor put it into perspective. "It was your mother's favorite. She hummed it all the time, too, even sang you girls to sleep with it. It's a tune Ophelia sings in *Hamlet,* dear."

Picking up the play and rereading it for the first time in years brought all the memories flooding back. Now when she hummed the song she could feel her mother's comforting touch, remember the way Trudy had eased her into sleep, even the night before she left.

Just thinking about the song and her mother made Miranda breathe easier. By the time she reached her studio, she found herself thinking about what to wear to an afternoon wedding.

"Isn't the church beautiful?" Winnie said softly the following day. Her aunt looked radiant in a flowered dress that made Miranda feel positively frumpy in her navy skirt and long-sleeved lacy white blouse. "Of course the bride is lovely, too," Winnie went on. "I introduced them, you know."

"That doesn't surprise me. Matchmaking is the

only hobby you put more effort into than your roses." She noticed that her aunt didn't bother to deny that, just smiling to herself and pointing out the beautiful floral swags at the end of each pew.

When was the last time she had come to Unity Christian Church and truly paid attention to her surroundings? She'd been too overwrought during her mother's funeral to notice much. The relief days later that it hadn't been her mother they'd buried hadn't brought back any details of the event. The sanctuary looked different somehow, and not just because of the lavish decorations for the wedding. Maybe the new pastor had made some changes.

She made a mental note to ask Winnie to introduce her to Reverend Brown after the wedding. The church glowed, showing the love and care the parishioners put into the old building, and certainly he had something to do with that.

The organ music changed slightly in intensity and the guests seemed to hush together as a door near the front of the sanctuary opened and a line of men filed out. Miranda recognized the groom as being someone in Bianca's class in school years ago. What did his young bride see in him? Miranda wondered.

He must have fine inner qualities, because any of his groomsmen were more handsome. The one at the end of the male parade was the most striking with his sandy hair and bright smile. Miranda gave herself a little shake when the good-looking "groomsman" crossed the sanctuary in back of the groom and positioned himself in front of the altar, facing out. Her cheeks flushed at the thought she'd apparently been admiring Reverend Brown.

She didn't have long to stew about it because the bride's attendants started their march down the white-runnered main aisle, led by an adorable little flower girl. Watching her, Miranda could imagine someone just as cute sprinkling rose petals from Winnie's garden in front of Portia. Was Mick's daughter Kaitlyn too old at six for such a role? Miranda was drawn away from that thought by everyone standing as the bride was walked down the aisle by her father.

For a moment she felt her chest tighten, thinking about how her family would handle the same situation. Would Ronald be able to walk Portia down the aisle, and would she even expect it? But before more doubts crept in, Miranda felt her attention drawn to the front of the church. Reverend Brown's entire attention seemed to be on the flower girl with her basket of petals. With a smile that captivating he had to have a soft heart for children. Miranda felt her cheeks color as she caught herself wondering what it would feel like to have that smile focused on her.

This won't do at all, she told herself silently. She was supposed to be here to make a practice run for Portia's wedding. Certainly that didn't include admiring the man presiding over the service. Miranda marveled at how deep her fog of sorrow must have been at the funeral to have absolutely no memory of the man's presence.

As the ceremony continued she found she couldn't pay attention to anything but Reverend Brown. What was his first name, anyway? She looked down at the printed folder in her hands, trying to ease it open past the cover adorned in white roses, ribbons and doves. There on the first page after the listing of the soloist and the Bible verses the couple had chosen was the line that read "Reverend Gregory Brown, officiating."

Gregory. A nice strong name. Looking back at the minister again, Miranda wondered if his friends called him Greg. Somehow the nickname sounded too informal for him in her mind. The man presiding over this wedding, now to the part where the couple exchanged rings, looked more like a Gregory to her. "Are you all right, dear?" she heard Winnie whisper in her ear.

"Just fine," she told her aunt. "Where did you say the reception was again?"

"I didn't. But it's going to be a lovely event on the lawn at the bride's parents' home. I hear they've rented the largest blue-and-white tent ever seen in Stoneley. And they're using the caterer I think Portia and Mick should look at first."

"Then of course we have to go," Miranda murmured, a little distracted by the brilliant smile

Gregory Brown gave the newly married couple as he presented them to the assembly as "Mr. and Mrs. Franklin" for the first time. They looked so incredibly happy. Miranda couldn't help smiling herself as they walked down the aisle together, grinning like two people in love.

Haunting and lovely. It was the only way to describe the woman on the bride's side of the church. Greg didn't know when he'd had to pull his attention away from a wedding guest and back to the couple being married this many times during a ceremony. Surely not since the second or third wedding of his career when the parents of those two-year-old twins had both been attendants and their little darlings had spent the entire service racing up and down the front pew from end to end over their harried grandmother.

At least this time his attention had wandered for more pleasant reasons. The beautiful young woman sitting next to Winnie Blanchard had to be one of her nieces. He remembered most of the family from the funeral he'd officiated at this spring. At that time all of Ronald Blanchard's daughters had been so grief stricken that their sorrow was what he'd noticed about them.

Today was a different story. For a change he actually looked forward to the receiving line. Certainly Winnie would introduce him to her niece.

She had such a doelike quality about her with those large dark eyes and even darker glossy brown hair caught up demurely in a twist.

Still fixated on the young woman who was leaving the sanctuary with her aunt, Greg was reluctant to pay any heed to the tugging at his elbow getting more and more firm. "Reverend Brown?" It was the officious photographer again; the man must have had dreams of a career in Hollywood. "We're almost ready for the family photos at the front of the church if you want to straighten up a little before that."

"But what about the receiving line?" Greg asked, his attention still on the Blanchard woman.

"Oh, no. That is terribly passé. Photos, digital video and off to the reception," the photographer said, all but clapping his hands in command.

Greg Brown's disappointment almost let him tell the man what he thought of his digital video, but he pulled himself together to present behavior fitting the senior pastor of Unity Christian Church. Besides, the quicker they got this over with, the quicker they could all move on to the reception where he could see Winnie and her lovely niece again.

TWO

"You're right," Miranda admitted to her aunt. "This is the largest tent I've ever seen outside a circus." It felt like acres of space inside the airy blue-and-white canopy, all of it taken up by a sea of white tablecloths on round tables for eight. Miranda scanned the nearest table, looking for place cards.

Winnie waved a hand at her. "Don't worry about finding our place, dear. I'm sure I can do that. Why don't you go take a moment to freshen up and I'll meet you back here in a bit."

Sweet, motherly Winnie was always looking out for her. Miranda nodded and picked her way through the tables until she found one of the smaller tents set up to cater to the female guests who wanted to relax a moment, check their appearances and otherwise take a breather.

She tried not to grimace as she looked at herself in the mirror. Her heavy hair never stayed as smooth as she wanted it to, and her mouth always looked too wide when she put on anything besides clear lip gloss. Sighing a little, she opened the navy clutch bag she carried to find the small pink bag holding her tiny collapsible hairbrush, lip gloss and the lace-edged handkerchief Winnie always insisted she carry. The handmade bag was just another reminder of how much Winnie had taken care of her over the years. Its fine-wale corduroy was faded and worn now, but Miranda would never let it go. Finding the rose lip gloss, she refreshed the color and gave herself one more critical glance in the mirror before leaving.

Since Winnie was finding their places, Miranda stopped by one of the tables where teenage girls who must be relatives of the bride were pouring cups of punch. She picked up some for herself and her aunt. It looked refreshing on this day beginning to turn warm under the tent. Weaving her way through the crowd, Miranda scanned the tables for Winnie. Near the front she spied her waving discreetly.

"Oh, good. You brought us some punch. Set mine down here." Winnie patted the place in front of her. "You're on my right."

Miranda looked at the place card where Winnie pointed. "How interesting. My name is written in the same calligraphy as everyone else's. Now how do you suppose they did that when I only agreed to come this morning?" She watched her aunt to see what her answer would be.

Winnie's cheeks turned a bit rosier, and she smiled impishly. "Well, I may have mentioned your name when I told them I'd be coming. I thought that perhaps you or Portia might accompany me. At least I hoped so."

"That's fine, Aunt Winnie. I wasn't accusing you of anything, just curious."

"Healthy curiosity is a good thing," Winnie said. "In fact I'm glad to see you interested in something outside the realm of poetry or your family for a change."

Before Miranda could open her mouth to argue about her interest levels, Winnie appeared to be focused on something behind her instead of what she was going to say. "Well, there you are, Reverend. What a delightful wedding. I'm so happy that we happen to be sitting at the same table."

Miranda turned to see Reverend Brown no more than three steps behind her. His smile was even more interesting from this distance, and up close she could tell that his eyes were a warm, deep brown. His dark suit and crisp white shirt rivaled anything one of her father's executives might wear, along with a tie that appeared to be nearly the same shade of blue as the bridesmaids' dresses.

"I couldn't wish for any better company, Miss Blanchard. And do I remember that this is one of your nieces?"

"Very good. Your ability to recognize people

after only a brief meeting always impresses me. But then, I suspect it must be a part of your job."

"That it is, Miss Blanchard. But I'm still at a disadvantage, because I have to admit that I don't remember which of your lovely nieces this might be."

"Please, I've asked you repeatedly to call me Winnie. And if you want to have a formal introduction, please allow me. Gregory Brown, I'd like to introduce my niece Miranda. You haven't had the opportunity to truly meet before, so I took the liberty of changing her place card for mine so that perhaps you two could get better acquainted."

He has a nice laugh, too, Miranda thought. It made the skin around his eyes crinkle in a charming fashion.

"Winnie, you continue to surprise me each time we talk. And Miranda, it's very nice to meet you formally. I hope you'll excuse me for a few minutes while I do some official things. I look forward to getting to know you much better when I return."

"Definitely, Reverend Brown." Only when he stepped back and walked toward the head table did Miranda realize that during the introductions he'd taken her hand. His touch felt so right that she only noticed when he let go.

In a moment he had a microphone and effectively silenced the buzzing crowd of wedding guests with just a few words. "Weddings were important to Jesus. We know that because he began his public ministry at a wedding reception. I'm sure you'll join me in welcoming the people who made today's reception possible by inviting all of us to share their joy. Ladies and gentlemen, let's thank Deborah and Jim Franklin."

A burst of applause and good wishes greeted the happy couple just entering the tent. Once they made their way to the head table and got seated, the minister quieted the guests again and said a brief but eloquent table grace. Afterward he turned the microphone over to the best man. Miranda was sure that whatever the best man said was probably charming, but she didn't really hear it. Instead she watched as Gregory Brown made his way back to the table. His progress was slowed by four different women making conversation. Even though they were too far away for her to hear what was said, Miranda was impressed by the pastor's apparent skill in speaking with each.

When he got back to the table, Winnie and Miranda had introduced themselves to the other guests at the table—a family of the bride's cousins who had traveled from Vermont for the wedding. Miranda found herself wondering just how creative Winnie might have gotten with the place cards, as there was an empty seat on the other side of the minister, and next to that the youngest of the cousins' family, a boy who looked about nine.

Then Gregory was there again, standing behind his chair, introducing himself to the cousins. He sat down next to Miranda, a wry grin on his face. "Sorry about that. Somehow it always seems to take longer to finish these little duties than I expect."

"That might have something to do with the fact that your progress was so impeded by congregational well-wishers—all of whom seem to be the mothers or other relatives of women I recognize from the area. Young, single women, I might add."

"How observant of you, Miss Blanchard. I must admit that you're right. There do seem to be many people concerned that I meet their friends and relations, all of whom are coincidentally women under the age of thirty-five."

"Hmm. Could it be that your congregation believes you might need a companion?"

His answering smile was the warmest yet. "It's quite possible. And if that is true then I must say that your aunt is the greatest believer of all."

Miranda had never felt such relief at the sight of a server with a tray full of salads. The bustle of the first course gave her enough time to cool the flush in her cheeks before she made any more conversation with the quick-witted Reverend Brown.

By the time the servers were clearing the empty plates after the main course, Miranda found herself charmed into talking with the minister again. Not that she'd been able to avoid doing so all through dinner, but she had been a bit on her guard. She just wasn't used to pleasant, handsome men sitting beside her and making her feel as if she were truly interesting.

Gregory Brown seemed to have that knack with everyone, Miranda decided. During dinner, he'd drawn out the boy sitting on the other side of him, discovering how the wiggly redhead would be spending his summer. Once he learned that young Jack was going to a church-sponsored camp, they discussed lanyard making, canoeing and whether mosquito bites or poison ivy was the worst scourge of campers.

"Sounds like you have a bit of camp experience," Miranda remarked once the plates were cleared and Jack and his sister had left the table in search of other cousins to hang out with before the cake was cut.

"A fair amount. I had a few years of scout camp when I was in grade school like that young man, and later I worked as a camp counselor a few summers in high school and college. How about you?" Light danced in his dark eyes. "Somehow you don't look like the camping type to me, but I could be mistaken."

"No, you're perfectly right on that one. My father and grandfather didn't approve of us going to camp, so we didn't. I might have liked to go somewhere that featured horseback riding when I was Jack's age, but soon after that was when we lost our mother and came back to my grandfather's house in Stoneley."

"Ah. Sorry to have touched on a sore subject,

even by accident." He looked so solicitous that Miranda believed him. It made her want to try to put him at ease.

"Reverend Brown, if you avoided every topic of conversation that might remind someone of misfortune, I have no idea what you'd talk about, do you?" With Miranda's family, so many paths led down those roads to despair she couldn't imagine how to avoid them all.

"There are still quite a few subjects we can discuss, Miss Blanchard. There's this wedding and the joy surrounding it, the beauty of the sunshine and the rest of God's creation around us, and what creative ways I can come up with to avoid being part of the lineup when Jim Franklin tosses Deborah's garter in a bit."

"But if you refuse, think of how disappointed all those lovely matchmaking ladies you talked to earlier will be at your lack of participation."

"Not half as disappointed as I'll be if I let myself be dragged into that," the reverend said. "No matter how far back in the pack I move, it seems that silly thing heads my way."

"Maybe we can do a little favor for each other then, and when the time comes we'll profess to be in such deep conversation with each other that you don't have to be in the garter parade and I'll avoid the bouquet toss." Miranda wrinkled her nose.

Greg's answering laugh was short but warm. "Not a big fan of the tradition either, I take it?"

"No, and not a believer in the impossible either. Since I'm unlikely to ever marry in the first place, I don't like to call attention to my still-single state."

Greg lifted a hand, index finger pointing skyward. "Well, if that's all it is, let me convince you that there's no such thing as 'impossible' for God. He delights in doing the things we call impossible, and does them on a daily basis."

"You know, Reverend Brown, you say that with such conviction I'm almost inclined to believe you."

"Please, call me Greg, or at least Pastor Greg. I hate to stand on formality with someone so entertaining to talk to. And I hope that we can talk more at length soon, Miss Blanchard, so that I can get you to remove the qualifying 'almost' from that sentence. At least, where the subject of what God can do for us is involved. I imagine it might take another conversation or two for you to be inclined to believe me on other topics."

The man was astute and direct. Miranda found herself smiling again. "Fine, Pastor Greg. But if I'm to be less formal with you, then I must insist you call me Miranda instead of 'Miss Blanchard.' For me that's Aunt Winnie, and although I seem to have cemented my position as the family's maiden aunt, I'm not ready to put myself on her level yet."

"I heard that part about maiden aunts, Miranda," Winnie said, coming back to the table after a visit with another parishioner at a nearby table. "And perhaps I can hand that title of 'Miss Blanchard' off to you some day. After all, I'm not so old that I'm destined to keep it forever."

For the second time in an hour, Miranda found herself rendered speechless by one of her table companions. "My goodness. Are things that serious with Tate?" Tate Connolly had just come back into Winnie's life after over forty years of silence. Miranda knew they'd been seeing each other, but talking about a wedding was news to her.

"Should I leave room in my schedule for premarital counseling?" Greg Brown flashed a smile that made Miranda's chest flutter.

"Not yet, but I'm hopeful I'll make that call eventually." Winnie's answering smile was sweetness itself. Miranda shook her head. Maybe Aunt Winnie was right in telling her she needed to get out more. If today was any indicator, she could use a lot more practice when it came to the fine art of conversation.

Mercifully, the rest of the reception passed without Miranda making more forays into any verbal minefields with Winnie or Pastor Brown. The rest of the conversation managed to be pleasant but inconsequential. Thirty minutes later she found herself looking at the small white box in her hand in bemusement. Winnie unlocked her car and settled her own box, handbag and other accoutrements in the back seat. "You know, when I was a girl they always told us that if we slept with wedding cake under our pillow we'd dream of the man we were to marry."

Miranda slid into the passenger seat, still cradling the small cardboard container with one slice of cake in it and the happy couple's names and wedding date inscribed in gold on the top. "That sounds rather messy, don't you think?"

"It most certainly does. That was one of several reasons why I didn't ever do it. Of course back then I was also sure that Tate Connolly and I would never get married, thanks to my father's disapproval." Winnie was quiet for a moment, and Miranda found herself wondering what it must be like to love a man for over forty years without the hope of marriage and a home of one's own.

"I have to gather from what you said back there at the table that you're not quite so positive anymore," Miranda remarked.

Winnie backed the car out of its spot and got on the main road headed for home before she answered. "No, I'm not positive anymore that I'll stay single forever. As that dynamic young man back there is so fond of saying, nothing is impossible with God. If I'm to believe that's true, then I have to think that God can find a way around my father and his hatefulness, and the bitterness it caused in Tate for so many years."

After that they were silent in the car for quite some time. Winnie's words kept echoing in Miranda's head, especially the part about nothing being impossible with God. Faith and hope seemed to have brought the right men into her sisters' lives, and instilled another kind of hope in all of them— the hope that Trudy might still be alive after all. Miranda so wanted to share that hope, and today she felt as if she could.

Before she knew it, Miranda found herself back on the wide circular driveway in front of the house, stepping out of Winnie's car with the box of wedding cake still in hand. Back in her room, changing into more comfortable clothing, she looked at the clock and did a double take. It was after five o'clock; they'd been out of the house for the better part of six hours and she hadn't even had the hint of a panic attack. Where had the peace she'd experienced all afternoon come from?

Miranda unfastened the clip holding her hair in its elegant pulled-back style and brushed out the wavy masses as she eased the kinks in her neck. Perhaps she could truly believe that things were possible for God. Maybe she could entertain the vaguest hope that someday she'd have her own home outside this forbidding stone mansion. There might be a life out there for her that included more than being everyone's favorite aunt, like Winnie, and spending her days alone in her studio.

She could see her eyebrows knot in the mirror as she pulled the silver brush through her hair. *That is a lot to hope for,* she thought. With her puny amount of faith perhaps it was too much to consider. Maybe she should start with something smaller, like going more than one day without the panic attacks that kept her virtually imprisoned in her home. And maybe she could daydream a little about something much less grand than marriage and a home of her own, but still satisfying.

Maybe, she thought, she should contemplate meeting the compelling Pastor Brown again soon. She gathered her hair into a loose band at the nape of her neck and reveled in the release of removing her dressy sandals. Wiggling her toes on the cool surface of the hardwood floor felt delicious.

Thinking about meeting Gregory Brown in the near future made her smile to herself. And just maybe the next time they met, the meeting could be more intimate than within the confines of a tent with several hundred people in it. Considering an actual date after one meeting was much too unrealistic, and more forward than Miranda could imagine.

Still, her newfound optimism certainly made the rest of her evening in the studio, hand-sewing bindings for that limited edition of books, go by in a flash. And, she had to admit, remembering the young minister's warm smile and even warmer brown eyes helped the time pass as well. Only after finishing her work, setting her studio in order and getting ready for bed in her room did Miranda realize something more startling than anything else that had happened all day. She hadn't hummed her mother's lullaby at all today, not one note.

"Thank you," she whispered to God as she drifted off to sleep. That night she dreamed of possibilities yet to come.

THREE

Journal entry
June 3

He's free! My darling Ronald got released from
jail. Now maybe that legal team that is costing him
so much money can go to work and get the ridiculous charges dropped. Isn't it obvious to everyone
that he wouldn't stoop to murdering a woman like
that? A person like her wouldn't be worth the effort.
Now that they have released him maybe we can
plan a lovely future together. I know he's only pretending to ignore me right now. As soon as it's safe
he'll be by my side.

"Remind me again why I didn't take the day off,"
Greg Brown said, sifting through the stack of messages the church secretary put on his desk.

"I have no idea," Janice said, her curly hair

bobbing around her slightly rounded cheeks as she shook her head. He almost expected her to cluck at him in disapproval, mother hen that she was. "You did a wedding on what's usually your day off, and then went home and did who-knows-what until late at night."

Is it that obvious? he felt like asking. Six months ago he would have asked, but now he knew that Janice's perceptions were right on target, even when no one else noticed something. "Now how do you know I didn't go straight home and go to sleep early, like I usually do on Saturdays?"

"Because you dragged in here this morning with the largest cup of coffee the Beaumont Beanery sells and now it's half-gone and you still don't look all that perky. What kept you up, anyway?"

"If I said working on yesterday's sermon some more, would you believe me?"

Janice made a huffy noise. "Not likely, unless the wedding provided some last-minute inspiration. Otherwise I know you, Pastor Greg, and that sermon was polished to perfection by Friday afternoon."

Ouch. She had him there. Janice had been the church secretary at Unity for so long that there were people in town who were sure they'd built the big brick church around her. She'd been invaluable helping him get settled in at Unity, and around Stoneley.

He wasn't going to tell her that he'd gone to bed

at a decent hour, but sleep had been elusive. All he could see when he closed his eyes was a woman with masses of dark hair and vaguely troubled golden eyes. Funny how Miranda Blanchard had entered his thoughts so thoroughly after only one real meeting. All morning Sunday he'd anticipated seeing her again, only to be disappointed when neither Winnie nor her charming niece came to services.

"You should have at least taken the morning off," Janice chided. "That way you would get in one of those long hikes you like to take, or go digging around in the archives at the county Historical Society. Although why you like rooting around there is beyond me. If I did that my allergies would act up so fiercely I would be sneezing for a week."

"Studying history is fun, Janice. It relaxes me and invigorates me at the same time. I want to know more about that Revere bell in the steeple and what it meant to the people who gathered together the funds and determination to put it there. I want to know more about the men of God who were here before me and how they got here," he said, raising his hands to take in his comfortable office.

"If you say so. Why don't you just read the book Muriel Whitby put together for the one-hundred-and-fiftieth anniversary of the church instead?"

Because Muriel's pamphlet is full of inaccuracies and it's boring, he felt like saying, but he kept his thoughts to himself. For all he knew Janice was related to dear, departed Muriel and his comment would open up a whole can of worms. Today he didn't feel like dealing with that kind of thing.

What he really wanted to do was sift through his dwindling stack of messages in Janice's neat hand-writing, wondering why none of them were from Miranda. Perhaps he could find a reason to call the big house outside Stoneley and talk to her. Hadn't Winnie mentioned that her father was still terribly ill? And surely the family needed comfort in this time of stress, with Ronald Blanchard in jail.

Will you listen to yourself? Greg felt so stupid he wanted to smack himself in the forehead. Did Miranda really need his self-serving attempts at seeing her again? With all the trials her family was facing already, the last thing she needed was another burden in the form of a man who had as many problems as she did…or more. At least Miranda had five sisters to support her and help her deal with the challenges in her life. For Greg, his only choice was to go it alone, and that wasn't working very well.

He looked down at the top message on the pile of slips. It was from his counterpart at the Presbyterian church across town, wondering if he wanted to give the program at the next Stoneley clergy fellowship meeting. Now this was more like it. Interface with the other clergy in town and building his ministry here at Unity was the business he should be about now. This was not the right time to work on his personal life, especially if that meant trying to get closer to Miranda Blanchard.

Sighing softly, Greg punched a number in his phone and waited for it to ring at the Presbyterian church. If this was what God wanted him to do, why did he feel so isolated? He didn't have an answer for that one.

"Can you believe he's coming home?" Portia said, sitting down with a thump on the love seat in Aunt Winnie's sunny library and sitting room.

Miranda shrugged, sipping her iced tea and fighting the urge to hum to herself. The events of the morning had her fighting off symptoms of panic, even in places like this room, usually one of her safest havens. "He hired the best legal team he possibly could. Bianca's recommendations helped with that. Did you honestly expect they'd let the head of Blanchard Fabrics sit in jail a moment longer than they could help it? Reputation is a huge part of the legal world, especially in criminal law."

"Yes, and reputation is everything to Father as well. He and his legal team must get along quite well together." Portia's dark eyes flashed. "Mick is so upset about this. He doesn't believe bail should have been set that low for anybody with access to everything Father has at his disposal."

Miranda found herself shuddering. "Does Mick think he's a flight risk?" At this point she didn't know whether her father leaving the country would be a blessing or a worry.

"I'm not sure. There are some things I'm not comfortable discussing. I don't want Mick to tell me anything he couldn't tell anyone else, including the journalists hounding him."

"I can understand that." Miranda patted her sister's shoulder. "This must put you in an awkward position between the two of them."

"Not really. After everything else that's gone on with this household, it's hard to have any sympathy for our father. Now Grandfather is a different story. As ill as he is, do you think he's noticed all the uproar?"

"I'm not sure. He's so sick I don't know if he's even aware that Father was arrested. I've kept my visits short this last week because every time I go in there it seems he's napping. Peg says he's still regaining his strength after the...poisoning attempt." Miranda had trouble even saying the words. Why would anybody give her grandfather poison, especially when it was obvious that only the watchful ministrations of his nurse and his family kept him alive and grounded to this world?

Nothing about her grandfather's poisoning made sense. At first Miranda, like the rest of the family, had just assumed that Howard had somehow over-medicated himself with one of his prescriptions during one of Peg's rare moments of leaving him on his own. Miranda knew it would be quite some time before the image of her grandfather unresponsive on the floor of his room left her. Maybe that was one of those things that Aunt Winnie would say showed God's hand in their lives. If Miranda hadn't chosen just that moment to go and visit her grandfather, the outcome of his illness might have been far different. At least now he was making some progress, even though it was slow.

Winnie bustled into the room, smiling to see her nieces already there. "I thought I might find you two here. And I couldn't help overhearing that last bit, Miranda. Sadly, I don't think your grandfather pays attention to much of anything these days. Of course my visits are even more limited than yours, so I'm not positive." Her smooth forehead furrowed slightly with consternation. "At least he appears to welcome my presence for short periods of time. For a while I agreed with Peg that I might be disturbing him."

Miranda rose automatically to give her aunt a brief hug. "If you disturb him, then everyone must be disturbing." She couldn't imagine her sweet, thoughtful aunt being a bother to anyone, even the confused, angry man their grandfather had become.

"You're kind to say so, dear. I just hope he doesn't have one of his lucid spells tomorrow and want to join us for dinner. I've invited Tate already and I'd hate to uninvite him. Now that your father is coming home today dinner might be uncomfortable enough as it is."

Miranda's chest tightened just considering the confrontations that might take place. She willed herself to stand still and breathe deeply. Maybe she ought to make sure that Portia and Mick would join them for dinner. Ronald and Tate might be on better behavior in front of the police detective engaged to her sister.

"Now that makes me glad that I've already got plans to take Kaitlyn shopping for a new bathing suit and out for ice cream afterward." Her sister laughed. "It's so nice to hang out with somebody who can eat ice cream without guilt right after trying on swimsuits."

Miranda found herself smiling. "It helps that she's only six."

"True. I guess at that age I wouldn't have worried either."

"You certainly didn't," Winnie chimed in. "And you wanted the brightest hot-pink one you could find, preferably a two-piece with sunglasses and flip-flop sandals to match."

"I'm surprised she didn't ask for a grass skirt to go with it," Miranda muttered, bringing laughter to the other two. She felt a momentary pang of jealousy watching them, both women calm and full of self-confidence. Winnie and Portia could each feel sure that they had the love and support of a good man. What did she have? Worries about a run of a hundred poetry books still unfinished and a huge, ongoing case of writer's block.

Nothing's impossible with God. Now why did that thought choose this moment to bubble up in her consciousness? It even came complete with an accompanying picture of Pastor Greg, laugh crinkles around those dark chocolate eyes just as they had been at Saturday's wedding reception.

Suddenly the room felt warm enough that Miranda grew uncomfortable in her wheat-colored linen shirtdress. Perhaps a little more ice in her tea might help. *Perhaps not thinking of Gregory Brown might help even more,* she chided herself.

How far outside the house could she go today without bringing on a full-fledged panic attack? It was worth finding out, just to take some action instead of sitting around entertaining visions of the good-looking Greg. "I think I'll refresh my tea and take it out to the rose garden," she said, deciding to push the issue. Maybe if she took a few of those books that needed to be sewn together she could distract herself from *all* the other things clamoring for her attention.

With a wide-brimmed straw hat and a lightweight white cotton long-sleeved shirt for protection, Miranda sat in the rose garden for hours while she stitched book pages together, then affixed them into their covers. The mindless work kept her busy and panic-free. She hummed her calming lullaby in time with the droning of honeybees around Winnie's roses.

The afternoon had proved perfect for being here in the garden. White, puffy clouds scudded by occasionally, but not the kind that threatened rain. The pile of finished books in the basket beside Miranda gave her a feeling of satisfaction.

"So there you are, Miranda." The familiar deep voice startled her and she gave an involuntary yelp as she stuck her finger with the needle instead of completing the stitch in front of her. She dropped the book into her lap quickly and put her finger in her mouth. The taste of blood repelled her, but bleeding on the book cover would mean she would have to scrap it and start over.

"Did you have to come up behind me and startle me?" Perhaps it wasn't a friendly greeting for her father, but she didn't feel friendly toward him right now to begin with. Wrapping a tissue from her pocket around her finger, she set the book aside on the bench seat of the trellis and stood up, glaring at Ronald.

"I'm sorry. I didn't mean to startle you. But I did think that perhaps you'd be glad to see me." His handsome face wore the expression of mild distaste he always seemed to have for Miranda. "I should have gone to the factory instead of coming straight home. Barbara might at least have expressed some appreciation that I was back."

Leave it to her father to be direct. If the events of the past few weeks had any effect on him at all, it might be a slight widening of the silver streaks at his temples. And he was right about one thing: if anyone would be happy to see him today it might be his loyal assistant Barbara Sanchez.

"She probably would have. Maybe it's not too late to find out." Miranda willed herself to breathe deeply as she looked boldly into her father's cold, dark eyes. If he had come straight here from his release, the authorities had given Ronald Blanchard plenty of leeway in jail. His tanned cheeks were clean shaven and he wore one of his custom-fitted charcoal suits with the white silk shirt Miranda knew came from Hong Kong.

"Ouch. How sharp as a serpent's tooth is the reaction I've got from my daughters today," he said, maiming a Shakespearean quote. If he thought that would make her or any of her sisters feel more generous toward him, the man had better think twice.

All she could do was shake her head. "Your daughters have real reasons to be thankless where you're concerned. You put your business before your family for two decades while lying to us and deceiving us about virtually everything in our lives. Now your fancy lawyers get you released on bail for murder and we're supposed to welcome you with open arms?"

Miranda felt surprise at seeing actual hurt in her

father's eyes. It wasn't an emotion she thought him capable of sharing.

"You don't think I actually did what they accused me of, do you?" Ronald said.

"Somebody shot Genie and left her on the floor to die. And with her dead we may never know for sure where Mama is now. If you didn't kill Genie, her death came at quite a convenient time for you."

"You have no idea what you're talking about. I don't have to stand here and listen to this." Ronald turned his back on Miranda and headed toward the house. "I think I'll take your earlier suggestion and go in to the office. It's obvious there's no welcome here for me."

"Okay, where are Your possibilities in this?" Miranda asked God softly as she watched her father's stiff retreating back. When he was gone she sat down on the bench again in disgust. The peace she'd felt before Ronald had interrupted her was ruined. And try as she might, she couldn't understand what even God could do with the impossible situation facing her right now.

FOUR

Journal entry
June 4

Why is Ronald ignoring me? I thought that once he was free again he would come back to me at once. His rotten, ungrateful daughters are to blame for his absence, I know. If only they'd all go away and take their foolish faith with them. Ronald can't really have had such a naive change of heart. He's only pretending to make them all happy. Perhaps soon they'll get the message and the prying will stop. Then their father would be back in my arms where he belongs. Unless something happens soon, I'll have to take action again.

After a fitful night's sleep, Miranda sat with a cup of tea at the breakfast table hoping that she could have a quick, quiet meal and slip off to her study.

Winnie normally took her own breakfast in the sitting room in her suite and sometimes Miranda joined her. But after last night's encounter with her father, she had felt more like hiding out on her own and trying to recapture the peace she'd felt in the rose garden.

Trying to write anything new had proved as fruitless as every recent attempt. She'd taken dinner alone just to avoid Ronald, even though it meant missing out on the company of the rest of the household, which might have cheered her.

Reading after dinner with soft music on the CD player had worked for a while, but in a short time Miranda could feel the tension building in her and the need to pace or just do something for the sake of doing it.

Normally in that mood she visited her grandfather. But when she'd gone to the door of his quarters, it was closed and her knock answered only by Peg Henderson opening the door the slightest crack. "Oh, dear, he's still just not up to company yet. He even shooed Sonya away when she came with his tea a little while ago," Peg told her, genuine worry apparent in her blue eyes.

After that the evening turned hopelessly dull, no matter what Miranda tried. Several times she found herself staring at the phone, wondering if she called Unity's office the message there might give her a way to reach Gregory Brown at home. It was almost possible to convince herself that the company she wanted from him was nothing more than pastoral counseling.

In the end she resisted her desire to make the phone call. Surely the pastor was so busy that he didn't need to be bothered with her problems. He had the entire congregation of the largest church in Stoneley to minister to, and compared to that Miranda felt like a drop of water in a pond.

With those thoughts swirling around her, sleep had felt as if it took forever to come. Now morning found her grumpily facing a rapidly cooling English muffin while she watched the birds outside the window, all of whom seemed annoyingly cheerful in the late-spring sunshine.

"That's no proper breakfast," her father said, setting down a cup of coffee and his *Wall Street Journal* at an empty place at the table, making Miranda wince. "Why don't you let me tell Andre to make another one of his special omelets for you and we'll eat together?"

"Thank you, but I prefer something other than those egg-white-and-spinach monstrosities, no matter how many nutrients you say are in them." Miranda started to rise from the table, but the wounded look in her father's eyes made her sit back down.

"Even if we can't agree on breakfast, I suppose we could sit together for a while," she said, wondering why she bothered.

The man actually gave a half-friendly smile and sat down. "Good. I feel we got off on the wrong foot last night and hoped that I could make a fresh start this morning. I even cut my workout short in hopes that I could get down here and catch you."

Miranda studied him as he unfolded his newspaper. The figure in front of her looked like her father, white shirt spotlessly crisp and dark suit pants creased to perfection. Some companies might have gone casual for their executive staff, but Ronald Blanchard didn't believe in such things. He certainly didn't sound like the father she expected. "What did you want to talk about?" she asked, trying to keep her tone friendly.

"Anything but where I've been since the police picked me up," he said, scanning the headlines. "I still can't believe they expected to hold me on such ridiculous charges."

"Is it so ridiculous to think that a man who was capable of faking someone's death for over twenty years wasn't capable of causing a death as well?"

"Yes, Miranda, it is." Ronald's black eyes flashed as he looked up at her. "You have to believe that I was doing what was best for you after Juliet was born. I would never intentionally have done anything that caused your mother that sort of harm. I only wanted her out of our lives where she couldn't hurt you."

"The way she hurt you," Miranda said softly,

aware that her hands shook as she put down her china teacup.

He winced. "I suppose you're right. Trudy was the love of my life and she betrayed me in ways that tore me apart. I had to take action." His dark eyes looked past the breakfast table and for a moment Miranda felt a pang of empathy.

It lasted only a few seconds before anger flared to replace it. "What you did damaged all of us far more than allowing Mama to stay ever would have."

"Oh, be reasonable. You were a child of ten, incapable of seeing how ill your mother was and how deceitful she'd been."

"That's true. I only knew that overnight the one person I loved more than anyone in the world, who would have given her life for me if necessary, vanished without even saying goodbye." She couldn't meet his face again, not with her eyes this full of tears. Staying at the table to talk to her father had been a huge mistake.

"Didn't I provide for all of you, even Juliet? Have you ever lacked for anything here in your grandfather's house?"

"We've never lacked for the material. You and Grandfather certainly wouldn't have let that happen as it would have been a reflection on your place in Stoneley society. What we lacked was a mother's love and care. And a father's as well, because you certainly didn't provide *that*. It's too late to think that a little chat over breakfast can make any amends for the years of neglect in that department." This time she found the strength to rise from the table to leave.

"And I'll regret that until I go to my grave," Ronald blurted, startling her into stillness next to her chair. "You can't believe how many times I've asked God to forgive me in the last few weeks for abandoning my children. I think that He can forgive me, Miranda. The question is, can you?" He grasped her wrist for a moment until she shook off his touch.

"I honestly don't know, Father." Miranda bolted up the back stairs toward her room, determined that whatever happened Ronald wouldn't see her crying one more time because of him.

Miranda felt like a butterfly pinned to velvet, drowning in the red plush, dark wood and gilt trim of the dining room of the manor as it closed in around her. If her father hadn't come home yesterday, the rest of them would probably be having a relaxing dinner in Winnie's library instead. All he'd done since he got home was cause trouble and stir up her life.

With Ronald home to preside over dinner, nothing would do except the cold, muffled silence of the dining room. Watching her father and Tate Connolly glare at each other across the table, she could barely choke down a spoonful of soup.

"The gazpacho is delicious, Winnie," Tate said,

never taking his eyes off Ronald. It made Miranda think of two big cats stalking each other. Her father was as sleek as a panther, while Tate bristled like a shaggy white tiger. "Knowing your green thumb, I imagine you have hothouse tomatoes someplace on the property that went into the making of it."

"It needs a little cilantro. And some pepper sauce," Ronald complained. "You shouldn't have had Andre tone it down for our unwanted guest."

"Now don't go aggravating your sister. It's fine just the way it is, Ronald." Tate patted Winnie's hand as he stared down her brother. "You've just burned out your taste buds with a few days of jail food."

Winnie put down her soup spoon forcefully, tossed her crisp linen napkin beside her plate and stood up at her place at the table. Being gentlemen, both men rose with her. "That will be enough out of both of you. Either be civil and pleasant, or don't say anything. You two are going to have to learn to at least co-exist for my sake." Winnie shook her head. "Honestly, you'd think that you were both raised in a barn."

Miranda looked from Tate to her father. Neither of them made a move to say anything to the other, or answer Winnie for a very long moment. "Excuse me, Connolly," Ronald finally said. "Our mother brought me up better than my actions are showing tonight. While we may have our differences in business, I'm willing to leave all that outside."

His statement made Miranda's eyes widen. Perhaps the reawakened faith he claimed was actually making a difference in his behavior. First he'd tried to mend fences with her this morning and now he had actually apologized to Tate.

Connolly's gray eyes flashed, and then he lowered his gaze ever so slightly. "I'll accept your apology for Winnie's sake. And for her only, I'll go along with that idea to keep our business competition out of her home."

Winnie sat down with a sigh and settled back into her place at the table. Wordlessly, the two men sat at the slowest pace possible, still staring each other down. The silence stretched to an uncomfortable length, broken only by the occasional faint chink of a silver spoon grazing porcelain.

Sonya had removed the soup bowls and brought in the poached salmon with new potatoes and fresh garden peas before anyone else made any conversation. She stood stiffly behind Winnie for a moment, watching her serve the delicate salmon fillet in dill sauce. "If there's nothing else for the present, I'll take Mr. Howard his tea," she said. Not waiting for an answer, she exited to the kitchen.

"How is your father, Winnie?"

Miranda knew that Tate didn't truly care about her grandfather's health himself. Given their history she'd even wondered briefly if Tate could have somehow had a hand in the poisoning that had left the older man so ill. However, watching Tate with her aunt in the past few weeks, she'd decided that while Connolly might wish to ruin Blanchard Fabrics as a company, he wouldn't stoop to injuring a sick old man who had so little time left on earth.

Winnie sighed before answering. "He is still recovering very slowly from that drug reaction." For the most part the family had chosen to gloss over the various ways that Howard could have been administered so much of one of his prescription drugs, bringing him to the brink of death. "I think his nurse, Peg, blames herself for his overdose, but I've told her that she can't be expected to monitor him every second."

"I don't know. We certainly pay her enough," Ronald groused, sounding more like the father Miranda expected to hear. "Whatever the cause, the old man is slipping a little more every day. I tried to visit with him this afternoon but it was hopeless. He kept asking me about my trip to Chicago."

"Ah. That's probably my fault," Winnie said, looking down at the tablecloth, her cheeks flushing. "I felt it was better not to upset him with the truth of your absence. The one time he asked where you were I told you you were away on business."

"It's good of you to protect your brother that way, Winifred. But then, you're the most good-hearted person I've ever known."

Miranda could hardly believe the tenderness that sprang to Tate's steel-gray eyes when he looked at her aunt. Maybe she would be inheriting Winnie's title as the family spinster quicker than she'd imagined.

"At least somebody is sticking up for me," Ronald said with a huff, breaking the light romantic mood Tate had managed to create.

Miranda could feel her chest tightening in the grip of mounting panic. How much longer could she stave off an attack with all this tension swirling around her? Was removing her growing anxiety one of those things that Greg Brown would term possible for God? She could hardly imagine that asking God to help her with her panic could work, but she prayed silently about it anyway. At this point she had nothing to lose.

Her prayer at least pulled her attention away from the contention at the table for a short time. She picked at her salmon, tried to regulate her breathing and prayed silently even though she felt terribly rusty at it. Before she knew it, Sonya had returned, removing the dishes. "Shall I serve the coffee and dessert in here, Miss Blanchard?" the housekeeper asked.

"Not just yet, Sonya. It's such a nice evening I was thinking we might move to the garden room," Winnie replied.

The more intimate space toward the back of the house had a pleasant view of summer sunsets, making Miranda almost wish she planned to stay. Instead, she rose from her place at the table. "I hope I won't disturb your plans too much if I excuse myself, Aunt Winnie. I got a call this afternoon from Fiber Arts in town that the flax twine I special ordered is in. The manager said she'd keep the store open until eight so that I could pick it up and I don't want to disappoint her."

"How about disappointing me?" Ronald grumbled. "If you have to make these silly little handmade books, can't you at least use products from Blanchard Fabrics to tie them together with, or whatever you do? At least we'd get a little free publicity that way when one of your weird poet friends has a reading."

Winnie looked at her brother, her lips pursed in disapproval. "Honestly, Ronald. Can't you just *try* and be pleasant to everyone for a while?"

Ronald made a disgruntled sound but had the decency to refrain from responding with one of his cutting remarks.

After a moment of oppressive silence, Winnie turned to her niece and smiled. "What your father doesn't seem to understand is the individual nature of what you do, Miranda. But then, he wouldn't normally know individuality if it bit him in the ankle."

Miranda felt a little of her discomfort slip away.

"In fact, why don't you go up to my room and get the keys to my car. It would be a lovely night for a drive into Stoneley."

Normally Miranda relied on one of the family cars with a driver, but she realized with a start that since she hadn't told anyone of her plans before this, no one would be available at this time of night. Sonya and Peg were the only staff members that always stayed at the manor; even Ronald's driver wasn't at his beck and call twenty-four hours a day.

"That's kind of you, Aunt. I think I'll take you up on your offer." Miranda said her goodbyes to her father and Tate Connolly and went up the broad front staircase to Winnie's rooms on the second floor.

She was in her own bedroom gathering up her purse, the solid weight of Winnie's keys in her left hand, when the feelings ambushed her, driving her to her knees on the plush rug. Suddenly there was no air in her lungs, and a cold sweat beaded her forehead. The keys slipped from her hand as she gasped, trying to focus her blurred vision.

"But I prayed!" she accused out loud. "Gregory said nothing is impossible for You. What did I do to deserve this?" She gave in to the tears then, sinking down on the rug, gripping tufts of it in her shaking fingers. For what seemed like half an hour she fought the anxiety, willed her chest to expand and let in air and heard her father's words ring in her ears. Words like "silly" and "disappointing" and "weird" that were all she'd come to expect from Ronald for the past twenty years.

As a young teen she'd come to terms with the knowledge that her father would never give her the love and approval most fathers had for their children. As the years went by she'd taken it more and more upon herself to be the target of his disdain, protecting her sisters from him when she could. Of course rebellious Delia rebuffed her efforts most of the time and the twins turned to each other.

Even when her sisters had all left Stoneley behind, Miranda had stayed, kept there now not just out of habit and custom but by the panic attacks like this one that blindsided her. She'd never be able to function on her own like this, and things weren't getting any better.

Weeping in frustration now over the sorry state of her life, Miranda acknowledged that she wouldn't be going anywhere tonight. Again. When she calmed enough to get up and wash her face she slipped down the hall to Winnie's room and put her keys back where they belonged. Taking the back stairs to avoid any contact with the household, Miranda went up one more floor to her studio.

Once there she didn't even turn the lights on; the wan moonlight felt like more than enough. Over in the far corner she sank down on the austere wooden bench she kept there, and leaned her back against the cool gray wall. She'd begun humming her mother's lullaby even before she'd totally settled onto the bench.

Cool and silver, the essence of the room surrounded her, letting the melody envelop her as she sought calm. It had been so long since she'd really had a mother to hum this familiar tune to her. When her mother was alive and with her, Miranda remembered having confidence and an adventurous spirit that had dwindled through the years until there was nothing left of it.

Resting her cheek against the cool wall, she sang the melody out loud now, not with words, but just sounds, as she remembered her mother doing to calm Juliet, who'd been a colicky, fussy newborn. She could see them in her mind's eye, the tiny infant restless in her mother's arms, the blond woman looking beautiful and tragic at the same time, walking up and down, patting the baby's back while she sang.

At the height of the melody Miranda broke off her singing, embarrassed by her need to make this memorial to her mother out loud. Trudy was still alive somewhere, she hoped. But if that was true, how would they ever find her? Miranda could feel tears on her cheeks. Ronald was right: she was silly and weak. The melody echoed in her head even after she'd stopped singing it.

At first she thought the cold that traveled through her spine was only her reaction to the chilled plaster under her damp cheek. In seconds, though, she shivered uncontrollably as she realized that the voice she heard wasn't a memory, but a real, human voice humming the lullaby where she had left off.

"Mama," she whispered almost inaudibly. Pressing her palm flat against the wall, she tried to *feel* the sound, find it for certain. When that didn't work and she was abruptly faced with silence again, she sprang up on the bench, rapping on the wall. "Hello? Who's there? Who's singing?"

For a few minutes she alternately rapped and listened until she became aware of her surroundings in a new way. She was standing on a bench in the dark, pounding on a wall while trying to communicate with a dead woman.

Suddenly fear swamped her in a way it had never done before. Panic under intense stress was one thing, but this was totally another. Ronald had always maintained that madness ran in the Hall family. Now Miranda felt faced with solid evidence of that. For what could this episode be but hallucination brought about by dwelling on her mother's memory?

"I need help. I need help so very badly," Miranda said softly, her words echoing off the walls. For hours she sat on the bench wondering where that help should come from, until she dragged her exhausted body back to her room and tried to sleep.

FIVE

Journal entry
June 5

I'm going to get even with those women no matter
what it takes. My dear Ronald is always so upset
and it's all due to those stupid daughters of his. No
matter how I've tried to get them out of the way they
still persist in their constant aggravation of the man.
I know what I have to do, but I'm not looking forward to it.

The next morning Miranda had tea and toast in her
room. Every noise made her jump. Was it real, or
something her mind had created to torture her? That
had to be the only possible answer to the singing
she'd heard the night before.

There was no way she wanted to be anywhere
near her father this morning. Even intimating that

she'd heard music that she couldn't find could mean that Ronald might figure a way to hospitalize her; after all, that seemed to be his answer to such situations. And maybe he was right. It certainly wasn't normal to hear voices when no one was there.

"This house is closing in on me," Miranda muttered. "I have to do something about that."

But then, what was the alternative? A panic attack caused by trying to walk out of the house was what had put her in this situation in the first place.

"Help me. I don't know what to do," Miranda whispered, not sure what she believed about the God she prayed to. He certainly didn't seem to be listening most of the time right now. Mental images of Winnie and her constant prayers sprang to mind. Maybe sharing all her problems with her aunt was the answer to her doubts right now. Winnie was the one person in the house she could tell about this without fear of their reaction.

Miranda dressed slowly, rehearsing what she'd tell her aunt. She didn't bother with makeup, but then she didn't normally use much. Lifting her heavy dark hair off her neck, she caught it up in a clip. She told herself that the face staring back in the mirror was pale and worried looking but didn't have the look of a madwoman. Taking a deep breath, Miranda left her room and headed to her aunt's suite on the other side of the second floor of the house.

Winnie's door was open, meaning that anyone was

welcome to enter her sunny sitting room or the sun-porch beyond. Miranda could hear soft music playing from the speakers on her aunt's bookshelves and see slight movement on the sun porch. Winnie turned from her chair outside and smiled. "There you are. How did your trip into town go last night? I hope you came to show me the things you picked up."

"Not exactly," Miranda said, crossing the room and coming to drop a quick kiss on her aunt's fore-head. "I didn't get there. In fact, I didn't ever get out of the house."

Winnie sighed. "Oh, dear. Things were so con-tentious at the dinner table last night I wondered how you might react. Are you feeling any better this morning?"

"No. I'm worried about last night." She sank down at an empty chair near Winnie, fighting tears. "Last night I felt worse than I've felt in a long while. The panic attack was monumental and it had some...new features that scared me."

When it came down to admitting that she was hearing voices, Miranda found that she couldn't tell even Winnie, whose sweet hazel eyes would hold nothing but acceptance no matter what she said. All her life her father and grandfather had impressed on her that only the strongest survived and prospered. If she admitted a weakness like this and they heard about it, what might they do?

What she'd already said was enough to worry

Winnie, and her aunt didn't need any more worries on top of what she had now. "Did Father and Mr. Connolly behave after I left? I had hoped that perhaps they'd be better if they were deprived of some of their audience," she said, trying to force a smile.

"They didn't come to blows at least." Winnie shook her head, causing a faded red curl that had escaped her chignon to bounce. "You'd think after all this time they could call a truce once in a while for my sake. I suppose I should be thankful that they've managed to tone it down."

She focused on Miranda. "But back to your problems, my dear. While we could spend all morning discussing Tate and Ronald and not solve anything, perhaps we might have more success where you are concerned." Her aunt's look radiated only empathy and love and for a moment Miranda felt tempted to blurt out everything.

The moment passed quickly before she said anything. "I'm not sure we can solve my problems either. I know Pastor Greg was quick to tell me that everything is possible for God, but Aunt Winnie, I prayed about this last night and I still couldn't leave the house. What could I have done to deserve this?"

Winnie reached a soft hand across the table to pat Miranda's. "Nothing, dear. That just isn't the way God works. If we got only what we deserved this would be a sorry, sad world. God delights in giving us so much more and I know He has something wonderful in store for you, Miranda. It just didn't include leaving the house last night."

Miranda saw that Winnie believed this fully. How did she have faith like that after all that had happened in her life? She could feel the tears in her eyes threatened to spill over. Talk about weakness. No faith, no self-control and a vague hold on sanity itself. It was all she could do not to put her head down on the table and sob.

"I don't know. Maybe coming here wasn't such a good idea this morning. How do you believe with everything that happens?"

"A very wise man once prayed, 'Lord, I believe. Help my unbelief.' That prayer has buoyed me up more than once," Winnie said softly. "The Bible says we only need faith the size of a mustard seed as long as we hang on to it. And you know how small a mustard seed is."

Miranda found herself smiling a little. "I do. You've shown me many times since we came to live here with you and Grandfather. You even gave me that necklace with a little globe with a mustard seed in it, remember?"

"Your twelfth birthday. Maybe we need to find another one," Winnie said. "Or do you still have that one?"

"I do. I keep it in…my makeup pouch in my purse." Winnie was the one person Miranda didn't have to say any more to about the worn pink corduroy bag. Her loving aunt had given her that, as well as a way to set a little girl free of at least one of the demons that haunted her. "I still carry the same one, you know."

"I know." Winnie's eyes were moist now, too. "But look at me, just sitting here and reminiscing when you need help." She got up from the table and went back into her suite for a moment. When she returned she carried a sheaf of papers that she set before Miranda.

"There. This month's church newsletter from Unity. They send it out now over the computer, but you know me and computers. I still print out the pages once I've downloaded them so that I can read the whole thing while holding it in my hand. I just get more out of it that way."

Miranda looked down at the pages, not sure what she was looking for. "That sounds like you, Aunt. But why are you giving this to me now?"

Winnie reached over and flipped pages until she found what she was looking for. "There, on the calendar of events. That support group you used to go to still meets there. Maybe it's time to go back and talk to the folks you were meeting with."

Miranda noticed how her aunt's direction had gently avoided any mention that the support group was for those with emotional illnesses, or family members of those with serious mental problems. She hadn't been to a meeting since January when things in the Blanchard household had started slowly sliding toward collapse.

Just thinking about having someone to talk to who wouldn't reveal her problems to her father gave Miranda's heart a little lift. The group had always been strictly confidential with each others' information. She suspected that at least half the people she'd met there didn't even know her last name. If they did, they certainly didn't give any clue outside their meetings.

She looked at the newsletter again. "You know, you might have a good idea, Aunt Winnie."

The older woman smiled. "Of course I do. Almost all of my ideas are good, Miranda. Surely you wouldn't argue about that?" Her aunt leaned down and gave her a reassuring hug.

"Not today, anyway. The group meets tomorrow night. I think I can hang on until then."

"Good. Maybe today we can have a little girls' day out together—go into town and get a manicure, drop by Fiber Arts while we're there and perhaps even have lunch at the Clam Bake Café. I hear they've changed to their summer menu and have a lovely roasted asparagus salad with blueberry vinaigrette."

"You've got a deal," Miranda said, grateful to have this sweet, loving woman in her life. Perhaps a day in town with Winnie would distract her from her problems enough that she could hang on until the support group meeting tomorrow night.

* * *

The next day and a half weren't exactly a breeze, but with Winnie's help Miranda found a way through them. Lunch out and picking up her supplies at Fiber Arts helped, because then she could spend her time working on the books she was putting together. Wednesday she woke up to soft spring rain but couldn't stand the thought of working in her studio again this soon.

Being there still made her listen every few minutes for the haunting singing she'd heard two nights before. She didn't think she could work there happily for the present, so she took the books she wanted to assemble to Winnie's sunporch. Sitting back from the windows she listened to the rain while she worked. Out here it sounded calming and smelled fresh.

Even when the rain cleared up mid-afternoon Miranda stayed on Winnie's sunporch. She felt safe there and only caught herself humming her calming lullaby once. But here on the sunporch she wasn't as worried about hearing the echo she'd heard in the night. In the daylight she could at least keep her fears at bay.

"So how many of those have you finished today?" Winnie asked, breezing onto the porch later. When Miranda looked at her watch she was surprised just how much later it was. She'd worked through the rest of the afternoon.

"I've only got about a dozen to finish the order," Miranda said, taken aback by her progress. "But they'll have to wait until tomorrow. If I don't get ready soon, I'll be going to that support group in my work clothes."

"I'm sure you wouldn't want that." Winnie looked over her reading glasses pointedly. "Shall I have Andre bring an early dinner up for the two of us in the sitting room?"

Miranda felt like hugging her aunt. "That would be great. I'll put these away and make myself more presentable." A quick shower and a judicious trip through her closet found her standing in front of her mirror much more pleased than she'd been in days. The dark green pantsuit was just the right weight for a night that promised to be a little cool. She twisted her hair into a set of inlaid wood clips and put on a little mascara and lip gloss.

"I appreciate the ride into town," Miranda told Winnie later as she sat in the comfortable leather passenger seat of her aunt's car.

"Are you sure I shouldn't stick around while you're at your group?" Winnie kept her eyes on the road, for which Miranda was thankful. "I could always stop by the library or catch up with a little of the paperwork at the hospital volunteer office."

"That's very sweet of you, but I think I can get a ride home with one of the other people in the support group. If neither of the women that I expect to see can help me out, I'll call you."

"All right, dear. I'll be praying for comfort and peace for you." As Winnie told her that, they pulled up into the parking lot of the church. Miranda looked around at the cars already parked there and tried to remember what either of her friends drove.

"Thank you for your prayers. You know they're appreciated." Miranda opened the door and slid out of Winnie's car. "And I'll be sure to call you if I need a ride home."

"Perhaps you could call me either way, just so I know you're all right," Winnie said. Miranda had to admit that her aunt was the only person she knew who worried more about her family than she did herself.

"I'll do that," she promised. Once in a while it was good to be fussed over. Being worried about like this almost felt like she had a mother. Miranda wondered what it would really feel like to have a mother's love as an adult. Would she ever know?

Greg Brown tidied up his desk so that he'd have a fresh start in the morning. Through the open doorway, Janice clucked at him. "You know, taking a night off once in a while wouldn't hurt."

"Says the woman who stayed late to finish up the newsletter and then headed over to a two-hour choir practice," he pointed out, which earned him a sigh and an eye roll.

"Now that's different and you know it. The newsletter is part of my job description. Choir is something I do because I enjoy it, just like everybody else in there. I really figured by now that you would have found someone else to replace Carleen. Her family moved to Boston at least three months ago, didn't they?"

"Four, but who's counting?" Greg smiled at her, trying to get his secretary into a more cheerful mood. "And how do you know that I don't enjoy leading this support group just as much as you enjoy choir? I did my undergraduate degree in psychology you know, and pastoral counseling is one of the few places I don't second-guess my abilities every fifteen minutes."

Janice finished shutting down her computer for the night, still shaking her head. "You're too hard on yourself, Pastor Greg. You're good at many of the tasks you perform as senior pastor. But how long will you stay on top of everything if you're here twelve hours a day or more almost every day of the week?"

Greg, having shut down his own computer, turned out his office lights and walked into Janice's outer office. "You've got a point there. I should be guarding against burnout. But I'll tell you a secret— I enjoy leading this Never Alone group more than I do a lot of other ministry groups in this church." He liked talking with the various members, sharing the ups and downs of their lives and watching the support they gave one another.

All in all this group of people with mental and emotional illness and their families felt like one of the most tangible ministries at Unity. "When I'm sitting in a meeting for an hour and a half talking about replacing the copier, it sure doesn't feel like ministry. But when I'm with this group the time flies by and I know I've made a difference in somebody's life."

"Okay, so maybe this wasn't the best example of where you could spend less time then," Janice conceded. "But I still think you ought to actually go out once in a while, maybe even on something like a date."

She snapped off the lights decisively and they walked down the hall together before going in their different directions. Greg wondered what Janice would say if she knew that the moment she'd mentioned a date a specific woman came to mind for him.

The image of Miranda Blanchard was still so strong in his mind that when he walked into the classroom where the support group met, Greg thought for a moment that the dark-haired woman in green facing away from him was actually Miranda. When one of the men called out a greeting to him and most of the people looked toward the doorway, Greg got a thrill of surprise. The woman was Miranda, and her golden eyes widened when she saw him.

Once more Greg was reminded of a doe in the forest when he faced Miranda. She had the startled look of a creature about to flee and he wanted to reassure her in some way that everything would be all right. But then he didn't know that for sure. It had been a good twenty years since anyone could have reassured him in that way about his own life and only God knows what kind of difficulties Miranda faced to bring her to this group.

As usual it took a few minutes for those present to find seats in the circle of chairs arranged near the center of the room. Tonight Greg struggled to remain mindful of his purpose here. Instead his attention kept drifting to Miranda—the way she hesitantly took a seat next to another woman in her thirties who Greg knew was there battling depression after the death of a child, and the way her troubled eyes seldom left him.

Get it together, Greg told himself silently. *She's only one of the eleven people in this room who needs your help.* No, Greg thought, there were twelve people in this room in need of help tonight and they were all seeking strength from the same source. Now it was up to him to point them all, himself included, toward the unimaginable love and compassion of that Source that was Jesus.

"Let's open with prayer and then we can start sharing with each other," he found himself saying as he sat down, Tonight, for a change, this meeting might not "fly by" the way he'd told Janice just a few minutes earlier.

Greg watched the rest of the group as they settled down to the normal routine of the evening. Several of them welcomed Miranda. He wondered how often she'd been a part of the group before he took over. He was tempted to ask her, but it was really none of his business. If she wanted him to know, she'd tell him, although he doubted that would happen. Miranda didn't have the look of someone who planned to talk much tonight.

As the evening went on it got harder and harder to focus on anyone but Miranda. Greg felt like offering the group an apology for his distracted-ness. But what was he going to say? That trying not to pay attention to a beautiful woman in obvious distress had his mind elsewhere? It was the truth, but it wouldn't help any of them to hear it. Instead he kept pressing ahead, saying little as moderator of the group and letting them help each other with their compassionate listening and caring.

He silently praised God for the reminder that it wasn't what he did as a pastor or even as a group moderator that made this session turn out as well as it did. Tonight he could feel the participants' aware-ness of Jesus in their midst, which made them reach out to one another to help the need they all had.

Listening to the stories of pain and hardship this group shared with one another always humbled him.

One man walked the daily tightrope of bipolar disorder, always trying to balance the cyclone of rising and falling moods while attempting to live a normal life. Another had an adult son who was a paranoid schizophrenic. "He's stopped taking his medication again, which means that he's likely to lose his job and his apartment and be back on the street in Portland." Greg's heart ached for this father and he told him so. Others offered the constructive ideas they had, but the group as a whole agreed that without court action there was little Bob could do about his son other than pray for him and visit when he could.

When Miranda spoke, her eyes full with unshed tears, Greg found himself holding his breath while he listened. "Bob, your son doesn't know how lucky he is to have a father who cares so much about him. I can't tell you how much I'd give to have my father care about my problems instead of telling me that I should just 'straighten up' and get control of myself."

"Are you still having the panic attacks?" the woman next to her asked softly, laying a hand on her arm in concern.

Miranda nodded, looking at a spot on the floor a few feet in front of her chair. Greg felt a pang of guilt, sure somehow that his presence here kept her from saying more.

"They're getting worse," she admitted. "Things have been so unsettled and my father snarls at everybody when he's home. There's only been one day in the past two weeks that I didn't have any problems at all."

"What did you do that day?" one of the others asked. "Maybe we can figure out what was different and help you do more of whatever it was that helped."

Miranda gave a weak smile. "I went with my aunt to a wedding here at church. Somehow I can't see myself looking for weddings to go to on a regular basis just to distract myself from my problems. Although with four of my sisters talking about getting married some time in the next year or two, and the other one a newlywed, maybe you've got a point." There was gentle laughter and the discussion moved on. Half an hour later, when the group said a closing prayer and broke up, Greg found himself listening to Miranda and the woman next to her.

"I've got my husband's truck tonight and it's full of his work supplies," the other woman said. "If I could jam another person in I'd offer you a ride home, but…"

"That's all right. I'll just call my aunt," Miranda said.

Almost without thinking, Greg stepped up next to the two women. "I couldn't help overhearing you, Miss Blanchard. It would be no problem for me to give you a ride home. Besides, it will give me an excuse to get out of the building quickly. That would make Janice, my secretary, happy because she says I spend too much time here."

"I'd have to agree with her, Pastor Greg," Miranda's companion said. "I'll get Bob to help me clean up here, because I know he has a key to lock up the building. Why don't you take Miranda home and go get some rest yourself."

Greg looked back at Miranda and shrugged. "Looks like they've thought of everything. Is this arrangement all right with you?"

She still had that deer-in-the-headlights look, and for a moment Greg thought he was going to lose his opportunity to be with her. But then something in her eyes changed and she smiled briefly. "That will be fine. I'm ready to go if you are."

With no excuse to stay, Greg found himself heading to the parking lot with Miranda walking next to him. Not the way he'd expected to end the evening, but that was okay too. When he found himself asking if she'd like to stop off at the Beanery for a little something Greg wasn't sure where the question had come from. He only knew that her agreement to that as well left him feeling lighter than he had since…since they'd said goodbye at the wedding. He pondered that the whole four blocks to the coffee shop, wondering what to say once he got there.

SIX

Miranda looked around the Beaumont Beanery wondering why on earth she'd agreed to stop here. When she saw that Greg Brown was moderating the support group her first reaction was to bolt. But his welcoming look had stilled her panic and she had forced herself to stay to try and find the peace she needed so badly. Now she felt much calmer and she knew she wasn't ready for the evening to end yet.

"I don't normally come here," she told Greg. "Do you?"

"At least two or three times a week," he admitted with a sheepish grin that endeared him to her. If this was his most serious vice, Miranda could warm up to him. She definitely envied him a life where showing up at the Beaumont Beanery a few times a week was probably the worst thing he did in the course of seven days.

"So if you come here often, what would you recommend?"

Greg looked up at the menu. "It depends on whether or not you like coffee, and how you feel about chocolate and perhaps whipped cream."

"Coffee is all right, chocolate is even better, and whipped cream is an occasional treat," she said.

He leaned his chin in his hand, still studying the menu written on the chalkboard above the area where a couple of teenagers stood ready to work two large, hissing espresso machines. "Then how about a mocha freeze, decaf this time of night, of course? With a little whipped cream. Do you want anything to eat with it?"

Miranda shook her head. "That sounds like dessert all by itself, thanks. And if you order, how about letting me buy?"

He raised a hand in protest. "Oh, no. I'm an old-fashioned kind of guy. I wouldn't dream of letting a lady buy my coffee when I asked her out."

Asked her out? Miranda wondered how he meant that, but she didn't want to ask how he meant that. He had asked her if she wanted to go for coffee. But then perhaps he took a lot of people that he counseled from the church here. It was a public place without being too public; perfect for maintaining distance and still quiet at the same time. She looked at the recessed booth over in the corner. "Well, then, if you won't let me pay shall I find us a place to sit?"

"That would be great. I'll order and come join you." Greg headed to the counter and Miranda slid into the bench on one side of the booth. Looking at her watch, she realized it was probably time to call Winnie.

Her aunt answered on the second ring. "Are you all right, Miranda? Do you need a ride home?"

"I'm…fine," she told Winnie, aware that she really *did* feel fine right now. Being with her friends from the support group had helped and being with Greg seemed to be helping even more with her earlier panic. "And Pastor Greg will give me a ride home when we're done having coffee."

There was a short silence on Winnie's end of the phone. "You're having coffee with the pastor? How lovely. I hope you have a good time."

"We will," Miranda said, watching Greg make his way across the room. "If it gets too late I'll call you so you don't worry."

"I won't worry as long as you're with him, Miranda. We can talk in the morning." Winnie said goodbye, leaving Miranda looking at her phone.

"What's up?" Greg slipped into the other side of the booth with a questioning look.

"I think Winnie just hung up on me. I called to tell her I didn't need a ride home. She must trust you a lot because she's not waiting up for me."

"Wow. I hope I fulfill that trust. That's a tall order. I can't think of many people I hold in higher regard than your aunt. She's definitely a special person."

"We think so. She basically raised my sisters and

me. Once we moved back to Grandfather's house and my father went back to work at the family business, he didn't seem to have much time for us."

Greg's forehead furrowed. "He had a lot on his mind, I'm sure."

"Right, like faking my mother's death!" Miranda looked down at the table. "I'm sorry. You don't need to hear all of this. It's still hard for me to deal with what we've learned in the last few months. It's difficult to feel anything but anger toward my father."

"And I suppose I shouldn't make excuses for him. I just can't imagine a father feeling anything but love for his children. I always felt such love from both of my parents, and even more deeply the love that God has for all of us as the best of parents."

Miranda tried to still her emotions and not say anything awful. She got an extra few moments to calm down when the teenage girl who had made their drinks brought them over to the table. Once she moved away from the table, Miranda felt able to speak again. "You're lucky, then. I can't imagine growing up with two loving parents. What was it like?"

Greg's smile was one-sided and didn't reach his eyes. "I can't tell you much. My parents died in an accident before I turned sixteen. My aunt and uncle finished raising me after that. They did their best, and it was always obvious that they loved me. But they weren't my parents. So I guess we have a few things in common after all."

Miranda felt a pang of guilt. "I'm sorry. I spoke too soon. I can't just assume that everybody has had a better life than I have." She toyed with the straw in her frozen coffee, not ready to drink it yet.

"No, perhaps I did in many ways. My aunt and uncle loved me and I've had a very fulfilling life since then. I can't imagine what the struggles your family has been through lately must be like."

His kind brown eyes radiated such honesty and concern Miranda wanted to tell him everything. Instead she took a long pull on the straw in her frozen coffee and drew back afterward. "Ouch. Now I've got a headache right between the eyes."

"The hazards of frozen coffee." Greg took a sip of his. "You have to go slowly with it, like so many other things in life."

"Well said. It's not as profound as Shakespeare, but it's a good philosophy." She rubbed the offending spot on her forehead until it felt better, then sipped at her coffee as Greg suggested.

He shrugged. "I'm afraid I know a lot more Scripture than I do Shakespeare. Literature was never my strongest subject at school. My favorite reading material has always been nonfiction. I know a lot more about Maslow's hierarchy of needs than I do *The Merchant of Venice*."

"At least you could name one of Shakespeare's

plays. You'd be surprised how many people can't."
Miranda covered her face with her hands. "That
sounds so terribly snobbish."

"Not at all. I'd expect things like that to be important to someone who writes poetry for a living."

"Not for a living," she corrected him. "I'd make
a pretty poor living out of what I have published, or
even my secondary business of handcrafted books.
It definitely wouldn't fund the kind of life I've
become accustomed to in my grandfather's house.
In that respect I'm very lucky that my family is
wealthy and doesn't mind supporting me."

Greg set down his coffee again. "I think with
what you do for them, it's got to be at least an even
trade. You and your aunt seem to keep the household running smoothly and you're there for your
sisters whenever they need you."

Miranda couldn't help giving him a smile that
probably looked pretty cynical. "I'm there all the time
because I can barely make it outside the house, Greg.
Surely you heard me admit that tonight." She felt
better for saying it. Her admission was likely to quash
any faint hope she might have for this one outing to
turn into something like a date, but this man already
meant too much to her to keep things from him.

What happened next totally surprised her. Instead of reacting as she expected, Gregory reached
across the table and took both of her hands in his.
"Miranda, I heard every word of what you had to

say. In fact, it was a strain to pay attention to anyone else tonight." His hands were incredibly warm, making Miranda want to draw back because she knew hers were cold after having them around the glass that held her iced coffee. But she couldn't pull away. All she wanted to do was look into Greg's eyes and see the concern there. It felt so wonderful to have someone look back at her with genuine, positive emotion.

Miranda tried to think when she'd last gotten the feeling of love or concern not tinged with pity from anybody but Winnie. With her father she shared anger and aggravation within minutes of talking to him most of the time. Perhaps Grandfather felt nothing but love for her, although his illness and confusion usually drew a veil over his deepest feelings. And while she knew her sisters loved her they often squabbled like…well, sisters.

Now here was Gregory sitting across the table paying attention to no one but her, his hands clasping hers in a way that made warmth radiate through her even more intensely than that headache moments ago. The feelings brought tears to her eyes and for a change she didn't try to hold them back.

"Oh, now that was the last thing I wanted to happen," he said, letting go of her left hand and reaching into his pants pocket. He drew out a crisp linen handkerchief and handed it to her. "I seem to have that effect on women."

Miranda let go of his other hand and took the handkerchief. She almost hated to use it, neatly ironed as it was. When she wiped away the tears with the square of cloth she was aware of the scent of his aftershave, or perhaps it was just the essence of Gregory. There was a light touch of aroma that made her think of pulling clothes off the line outside with her mother when she was little, both of them laughing as the wind wrapped cotton sheets around them. Along with that was the scent of vanilla and a brisk spiciness. She dried her face before she gave in to the urge to bury her nose in the cloth instead.

"Thank you. And please, don't worry about me. Crying a little is probably the best thing I could do. Winnie says I bottle everything up inside and she's probably right. I've been doing it so long, trying to stay strong because I'm the oldest. Maybe if I hadn't done that, I wouldn't have so many of these panic attacks."

"It might be at least one of the reasons. From what little I know, the worst thing about panic attacks is the constant fear that you'll have another one."

Miranda nodded. "You're right. I'm constantly worried lately that I'll find myself out in public and be overcome by one." Just thinking about it made her chest tighten for a moment as she tried to push the feeling away.

"The only other thing I can say about that is I'm sure God wants so much more for you. In Romans, the Bible tells us that God doesn't give us a spirit of fear. It's just not what he intends for his children."

He spoke so earnestly and Miranda wanted so badly to accept what he said. "I guess that's why I'm not terribly spiritual. It's so hard for me to take in all the things the Bible says about God as a totally loving, accepting father. It's just so far from my personal experience." Her tears welled up again, more in anger and frustration now than anything else, and she wiped the handkerchief across her cheek. "I must look awful," she said, willing her voice to stop quivering. She laid down Greg's handkerchief and reached into her purse to pull out her zippered makeup bag. It took a moment to find the small mirror and lip gloss she knew she needed now.

As she got them out she noticed Greg looking at the bag. "There has to be a story to that. It's not at all the designer leather number I'd expect to find in your purse, Miranda."

Now she had to fight bursting into tears again, but the pastor looked so genuinely interested in her answer that she had to tell him the whole story. "Winnie made it for me about twenty years ago."

"It looks like a well-used treasure," Greg said, endearing himself to her for good. He could have noted instead that the pink corduroy was faded and thin in spots, and worn down past the wale by touching. Instead he'd noticed how cherished it was.

"You're right. It is the one link I have with my

mother that I can carry around every day." She fingered the cloth lovingly. "When I was ten my mother and father had a terrible fight and she left home. The next morning Father told us that she had been in an accident after she left and had died. Of course we know now that wasn't true, but for twenty-three years that was the story we all believed. For years I was sure it was all my fault."

Greg shook his head slowly. "That had to be painful. What could a ten-year-old have possibly done that caused that belief?"

"The day before she left, Mama and I had quite a disagreement. She had just finished sewing a pink jumper and white blouse for me to wear to school and she wanted me to wear them that morning. I told her they were way too girly and they looked like baby's clothes and I was never going to wear them to school when all the other girls wore jeans every day."

She smiled ruefully. "Of course, that wasn't all quite true. Not all the other girls wore jeans all the time, and I only thought the jumper was babyish because she'd made the same pattern in different colors for Bianca and Delia."

"But you felt guilty for arguing with her and you remembered that last argument after your father told you she was dead," Greg said softly.

Something in his voice made Miranda wonder how he knew so exactly the thoughts that had gone through a young girl's mind.

She nodded, still holding the makeup bag. "Somehow I wanted her to come back so badly that I got it into my head that if I wore that outfit to school maybe she would come back. Part of me understood death in the grown-up way, and yet there was still the little-girl part that wanted wishes to come true."

Greg took the bag from her, handling it as gently as she would herself. "Your aunt made this out of your jumper, didn't she?"

"Yes. I wore it every day to school for weeks until the other kids teased me about not having any other clothes. I still wore it at least one or two days a week after that, until I had such a growth spurt that it was too short. After that it became my security blanket and I slept with it under my pillow for a couple of years.

"My father somehow caught wind of that when I was twelve and threatened to burn it. When she saw how panicky his threat made me, Winnie spirited it away and promised me that she'd fix everything. For my thirteenth birthday she gave me this bag, filled with a tiny mirror, clear lip gloss and a few other things she thought a teenager ought to have."

Greg gave the bag back to her. When he spoke he sounded as if he had a lump in his throat. "And here I thought I couldn't have any more respect for your aunt. She certainly devoted herself to you girls, didn't she?"

"More than you can imagine. I know you've heard what everyone else has around town the last six months, but there's so much more to the whole awful mess." With the makeup bag still there in her hands, Miranda found herself relating the recent events and all the painful twists and turns her life had taken.

When she laid it all out there for Greg, including hearing the shots and finding the body they thought was Trudy in the library, all the disclosures since and then discovering her grandfather after the attempt on his life, it was a revelation. "No wonder I've had so many terrible panic attacks lately. I haven't told a soul about any of this."

"You've discussed it with your sisters, I'm sure, but they've been under the same strains themselves. Have you ever considered a therapist?" Gregory was holding her hand again, with those warm brown eyes focused on her as if she were the only other person in the world.

Miranda sighed and shook her head. This was more difficult to explain than the rest of the family problems. "Not really. Father always drummed into us that Mama left us because she was crazy. Any sign of mental weakness was to be eradicated immediately. He wouldn't even let any of us cry in his presence."

"Wow. I know that there wasn't nearly as much child counseling twenty years ago as there is today, but I gather that means none of you got any grief therapy or other help. That just isn't right."

"I know that now. But then we just accepted it because that was the way Father said strong people handled things. And the Blanchards were strong." She could still hear his horrible remarks about the problems on her mother's side of the family. "I heard that for so long that even though I know it's wrong, that nobody has to be that strong alone, it's hard to even think about seeking professional help."

"When you're ready to do something, I'll be here for you, Miranda," Greg said softly but with conviction. "And more than that, God is always with you. There's nothing we can suffer that Jesus doesn't suffer along with us. We're never alone, even in the darkest times."

"You really believe that, without even thinking about it, don't you?" The idea still felt foreign to her, but she could see that to Gregory it came as naturally as breathing.

"I really do. It's the most often spoken promise in the Bible. God tells us over and over that He will never leave us, that He's always with us no matter what."

Miranda felt the tears pooling again as she saw the worn makeup bag, her melting iced coffee and the scarred surface of the wooden tabletop. "Of course it's easy for you to say that, Gregory. With a life as perfect as yours, how could you not believe that?"

The words had hardly left her lips before Miranda saw how they wounded him. He drew back the hand holding hers and looked as if he was going to say something for a moment. Then his expression changed from hurt to something else, the light she'd seen all evening in his eyes shutting down. "I guess it looks that way, doesn't it? Appearance isn't everything, you know."

"No, not everything. But it's the only thing others are privy to most of the time," she said. The silence for the next few moments was heavier than their conversation had been before. She looked at the puddle of cold condensation forming around her glass. "I'm sorry for keeping you here so long. I think maybe you should take me home now, unless you'd rather I called Winnie to come and get me."

"No, I offered to take you home. But you're right, we should probably go," Greg said.

All the way to his car, Miranda berated herself for the way the evening was ending.

SEVEN

You know you're an idiot, Greg told himself as he walked with Miranda to his slightly battered little SUV. How had things gone so wrong so fast back there? He was supposed to be a pastor, a shepherd for the lost sheep and here he was acting like a spoiled kid just because Miranda had intimated he was perfect. Wow, what an insult. He struggled with his thoughts, trying to find a way to bring things back somehow close to where they'd been before that little exchange.

At the car he pushed the button that automatically unlocked all the doors, and then stepped to the passenger side to open hers. "Do you need any help getting up there? Even with the running boards it's kind of a stretch for some women."

"Thank you, but I think I can manage," Miranda said, her voice sounding a little frosty.

Greg wanted to protest that he'd be happy to help, but the truth was that Miranda was tall enough that she probably didn't need help getting up there. Still, he wished for the excuse to hold her hand because the action could begin an apology he still wasn't sure how to make. Instead he stood by the side of the door until she got in and then closed her door. Aunt Martha would blow a gasket if she thought he wasn't doing things like that for a lady. And Miranda was certainly a lady.

That was probably part of the problem tonight. He had no idea how to deal with this woman. She wasn't at all like anyone else he'd met lately. There was an air of vulnerability about her that made him want to protect her, yet she gave the impression of not wanting too much help. Greg started the car and pulled away from the curb, realizing he hadn't been to the Blanchard home in months and wasn't sure he remembered how to get there.

Turning down the gospel CD playing, he pulled over into the nearly deserted municipal parking lot. Miranda looked at him in surprise. "All right, I can't play the stoic male for the rest of the drive. I need directions to your house."

A ghost of a smile played around Miranda's lips. "Now there's a conundrum. I'm not sure I can call you perfect anymore. Admitting to needing help certainly gives you an imperfection. But a man actually asking for directions? That puts you closer to perfect in my book than almost any other man I know."

He had to smile along with her. When he did,

Miranda's shoulders sagged slightly. "Do you mind shutting off the engine for a little while? I feel like I really messed up back there and I want to try and start fresh with you," she said.

The shine in her golden brown eyes made Greg sure that he couldn't refuse her request. He turned the key and shifted in his seat so that he was looking at her. "It's as much my fault as yours, Miranda. I guess being called 'perfect' is a thorny issue for me. Ministers are always held up as this standard whose behavior must be spotless, and it gets to me. I mean, I'm a normal human being like anybody else and perfection isn't possible for me any more than it is for you, or your aunt Winnie or anyone besides Jesus."

"I suppose I know that, but you're right, I automatically put you at a level higher than me on my personal behavior scale. Perhaps I shouldn't have done that, but I suppose I just naturally expect you to be better than I am, after years of seminary training and the experience you've had as a minister. But I truly didn't mean to get you going like that, Greg."

Her hand was on his arm now and he could feel the warmth of her touch through his cotton shirt. The fingers resting on his sleeve had the delicacy of butterfly wings.

"There is a lot of anger in me right now," she continued. "I shouldn't have taken some of it out on you."

He shrugged softly, hoping her hand would stay

where it was. She didn't move and he luxuriated in her touch even though he knew he ought to pull away. "I'm fairly tough. It should take more than that to offend me. If I'd been thinking the way I should, I would have laughed it off."

"So you forgive me? And we can go back to being friends?"

Her eyes held such depth of feeling Greg leaned closer toward her, wondering if her skin would feel as velvety as it looked. It took all his strength to resist closing the gap between them and discovering that with his lips on her cheek.

His head felt as if it were spinning. What was there about this woman who drew him so? Normally vulnerability made him step back and go into "pastor mode" right off the bat. He usually wanted to try to fix the problems of those in need, but at a safe distance. Instead, Miranda made him aware that she was a woman in so many little ways, and unless he was badly mistaken she wasn't trying to do that at all.

He leaned back slowly into his seat, easing her hand off his arm with his motion. "Of course we can be friends." The struggle would be how to keep himself in a position where all he would be to Miranda was a friend. She certainly didn't need anything more, especially from somebody with even more problems than she had herself.

She brightened even more at his statement,

making him feel worse for wanting to keep his distance. "Good, because I could use a few more friends. I don't make friends easily, but when I do the relationship is important to me."

Okay, right about now was when the warning bells would normally be going off in his head. He was alone in the car with a beautiful woman who needed comfort and friendship. But this time all Greg could think about was how to give her what she needed without hurting either of them.

It was time to get things moving again. "Well, friend, how about giving me those directions to your house? I imagine we could both use a good night's sleep and I need to get you home."

Miranda's directions were concise and in just a few minutes Greg found himself at the gate of the Blanchard estate. She gave him a series of numbers to punch into a keypad and the gates swung open. They made their way up to the house and Miranda directed him onto a secondary driveway that led around to the back of the house.

"I usually go in this way, through the mudroom and kitchen," she told him. "I like using the back stairs up to my room because it keeps me out of the front hall and those formal public rooms there."

"You strike me as more of a family-room kind of person," Greg said, picturing her in an easy chair or curled up on the end of a comfy sofa with a good book, perhaps with a cat on her lap.

She gave a short laugh. "Would you believe that out of the fifteen or more rooms that this house has, there's absolutely nothing that could be called a family room? The closest we have is the study in Aunt Winnie's suite. My sisters and I have always gathered there, or on the sunporch off of it in the summertime."

Greg felt a bit sorry for anybody with all the obvious wealth of the Blanchards who had to deal with such poverty of family togetherness. He didn't want to say anything that would cause another awkward situation, though, so he kept his thoughts to himself. "I hope you'll let me see you to the door," he said. "I have an aunt, too, and if she ever thought that I had let a lady go into a darkened house without company she would be very unhappy with me."

"Well, we wouldn't want that." Miranda opened her door and started up the path to the mudroom. Greg started out a few steps behind her but caught up quickly with his longer stride. She seemed to be searching for her key in her purse. Once she found it she turned to him.

"Thank you for taking me home and for all the help you've given me this evening. I appreciate your leadership of the support group, even though seeing you there worried me a little when I first came in."

"Why was that?" Greg asked.

"After sitting at your table at the wedding and having such a delightful time, I was appalled that now the same man I had a meal with would know all my awful secrets." She looked as if she wanted to bury her face in her hands, and Greg was overwhelmed by the desire to make her feel better.

"Please, don't give it a second thought. Discussions in a support group like those are a part of what I'm trained to do, and I would never mention them outside of that meeting. Your secrets are safe with me."

Miranda's fingers trembled and she dropped her house key. Greg automatically bent down to retrieve it at the same time she did, and in trying to avoid crashing into each other he could see her losing her balance. Rising, he clasped her arms just firmly enough to keep her from falling. That brought them face-to-face, her breath so close to him that for a split second he could only pay attention to her nearness.

Overwhelmed by the attraction he felt for her, Greg closed the small space between them and kissed her on the lips. She was as velvet soft as he'd expected. The tenderness of the moment surged through him and it was all he could do not to wrap his arms around her and kiss her much more thoroughly.

It only took a split second for his conscience and common sense to take over and let her go. "I'm sorry. I don't know what came over me. Are you all right?"

She touched one finger to her lips with the expression of a sleepwalker woken from a dream. "All right? I think so. My key is still down on the walk, though, isn't it?"

"Yes. Do you want me to pick it up?"

"That would be fine," she said slowly. He found the silver glint of it on the bricks beneath their feet and picked up the key, handing it back to Miranda.

"There. And I need to apologize again for what just happened."

"Why? Do you regret it that much?" Her question threw him for a loop.

"Regret it? Only for your sake. I know that kissing you wasn't the right thing to do but I couldn't help myself." That sounded lame the minute the words left his mouth, but Miranda didn't seem to mind.

"Good. Because I don't regret it, either, even though it was totally…unexpected." She put a hand to her temple and Greg wondered if she felt a little dizzy. "Could we go sit down on that bench over there?" She pointed to a stone bench a few yards away.

"Sure." The bench felt cool to the touch but not cold. The smooth surface under Greg's hand made him more aware of his surroundings on the lush grounds of the estate. That brought home with force another of the differences between him and Miranda. He'd never had much in the way of money, even when his parents were alive, and this woman had grown up surrounded by wealth.

Miranda sat down and took his hand, putting

Greg's full attention on her once more. "Even though that kiss can only be a one-time experience it convinced me of something. I'm sure now of what you said, that my secrets are safe with you," she said.

She took a deep breath. "I've got a huge secret to tell someone and I hardly know where to begin."

"Just start telling me whatever you need to," Greg said, trying to keep his voice calm and even. "I'm not going anywhere unless you want me to." He squeezed her hand gently and she squeezed back.

Miranda felt so incredibly comforted by his kind, accepting presence. She fought to keep from crying. "Good. I know you heard me tell the group about how my panic attacks have gotten so much worse lately. That isn't the only reason I came back to the group." Now she was getting to the scary part, but she still wanted to push on.

"I had a feeling there might be more." Greg's gaze made her feel that he was the only person in the world. "What's happening, Miranda?"

Her first impulse was to say anything but the truth. *Help me, God,* she prayed silently. With a surge of confidence she kept looking straight at Greg. "Last night I had an especially bad panic attack and I went to my studio. It's the place where I can usually calm down no matter what. I know it sounds childish but I have a song I hum to soothe myself. It's a lullaby I remember my mother singing. And last night...I think I heard her singing with me."

She couldn't watch his eyes anymore. Surely his expression would change now and this wonderful connection between them would be over. The next words she'd hear would be Greg telling her that she was in need of serious psychiatric help.

Instead there was silence around them for a few moments, so deep that she could hear crickets in the grass. He let go of her hand, making Miranda's heart sink, but then his arms wrapped around her in an enveloping hug. "Oh, Miranda. This has been so hard on you. You're so sure that your mother is alive now, and near you. With all the stress of this situation, perhaps your mind is trying to give you the thing you want most...contact with her."

Relief washed over her like a wave. "You mean you don't think I'm crazy?"

Still in Greg's arms, she could hear his sharp intake of breath. "I'd never say that to anyone. It's just not a word I'd use even if I thought you might need medical help. But I don't think it's time to see a counselor just yet." He let go of her but didn't pull too far away. "If this happens again, though, I hope you'll tell me."

"Of course." She didn't have to think twice about it. "After tonight I feel that I could tell you anything, Greg."

Miranda wasn't sure if she saw the briefest flicker of a shadow on his face. If she had, it disappeared quickly. "I'm honored by that. I'll try to keep earning your trust. But right now, we probably both need to get some rest."

She was glad there wasn't too much light in this back garden. That way Greg couldn't see her blush. "Of course. I'm sure you have so much to do in the morning, and it's late. Thank you again for bringing me home. And for everything else." They both rose from the bench and he followed her to the back door. He stood there until she was safely inside, and only then did he wave and go back to his car.

Miranda locked the back door and leaned against it, watching as Greg started his car and pulled away. This had been the most amazing evening of her life. Now she had to bring herself back to earth and concentrate on the mundane things, like setting the security system Aunt Winnie had turned off since she'd been out late, and going upstairs quietly so she didn't disturb her aunt. Usually she would welcome a quick chat with Winnie when she'd been out somewhere, but tonight she needed to be alone. One look at her face and Winnie would have all kinds of questions Miranda wasn't ready to answer.

EIGHT

Journal Entry
June 9

I'm going to have to take action. My dearest
Ronald's daughters, especially Miranda and Portia
still won't let up. There's no way I can sit idly by
and do nothing while they continue to monopolize
all of their father's attention. Perhaps if I make them
see how aggravating they've been they will start
leaving him alone. I hope I don't have to do anything drastic.

*F*our rows back, second person in from the aisle.
Greg couldn't focus anywhere else during the early
service on Sunday. Ever since Miranda and Winnie
had walked in and sat down, his attention had gone
there first. Miranda looked beautiful in her rose-
colored skirt and lacy white blouse. Was she a

morning person? She looked a lot more alert at this early hour than he felt. But then he hadn't slept all that well since Thursday night.

Once the service started Greg tried to keep his concentration on almost anyone else, especially during his sermon. He had a responsibility to communicate the Gospel in the clearest way possible and looking at Miranda didn't help keep his head clear. Any more than a glance at that shining dark hair and beautiful face and his focus might falter. There would be plenty of time after the service to talk to Miranda and her aunt. Greg wondered whose idea it had been to have Winnie to invite him to lunch today.

He didn't know whether to hope it had been all Winnie's idea or not. He'd felt like a high school kid most of Friday and Saturday, staring at the phone, even picking it up to call Miranda once in a while before chickening out and putting it down each time. If only he knew exactly what to do.

Most of the time he wrestled with the bigger issues in his faith life, not the smaller ones. The little decisions got committed to God without even thinking. Until now God had provided a ready answer to every question in his life but one, and that one might take him this lifetime to answer…or not. Some days he was okay with not knowing the answer to his own personal "why" and some days it ate him alive. Still, until now, wondering about that night nearly twenty years ago was the only thing that stopped him in his tracks. Now he couldn't even figure out whether to make a simple phone call.

The hymns this morning weren't helping either. He sat after his sermon, singing "Have Thine Own Way, Lord" along with the congregation, mouthing the words while he wondered what that way really was. The song said he was willing to be the clay shaped by the Divine Potter but right now he felt more like Silly Putty. Didn't God want him to concentrate on building this church and ministry instead of wasting time on his personal life?

He looked over at Winnie and Miranda again, drawn like a magnet. Winnie sang sweetly, her voice lifted surely to God as she sat with perfect posture not even looking at the hymnal Miranda held. The older woman's pink cheeks matched the rosebud tucked in her high chignon, which complemented the shades of her chic floral dress. By contrast, Miranda seemed to be concentrating solely on the words in front of her, one wavy tendril of dark hair loose from the clip in back brushing her cheek. As the organist wrapped up the song, Greg sent up a silent prayer. *What is Your way for me? Does it include this woman?* And if it did, Greg wondered, what on earth did he do next?

A few minutes later he found himself at the back of the sanctuary, shaking hands with the congregation as they filed out toward the parking lot. He tried to focus on each person in front of him, from

ninety-year-old Grandpa Harrison with his squeal-
ing hearing-aid battery to three-year-old Katie
whose teddy bear needed a hug. Even so, he could
feel Miranda growing nearer even without looking,
until she and Winnie stood directly in front of him.

"That was a very good sermon, Reverend,"
Winnie said, clasping his hand. "Maybe you should
try listening to it some time."

Ouch. Did his lack of concentration show that
badly? He opened his mouth to say something, but
saw from Winnie's sparkling eyes and impish smile
that she didn't expect a serious answer. "Are we still
on for lunch?" he asked. Maybe deflecting her
would work.

"We certainly are. Do you need directions to
the house?"

"No, he brought me home just a few days ago,
remember?" Miranda broke in. "You can find us
again, can't you, Pastor Greg?" In contrast to her aunt,
she looked more serious, but not with the deep sadness
she seemed to have when they'd talked on Thursday.

"I know I can find you again, Miranda. Do you
mind if I go home first and change out of my work
clothes?" he asked, looking back at Winnie.

"Of course not. I didn't expect you to wear a suit
and tie all through Sunday lunch," she replied. "It
will just be the family today, and I'm not sure all of
us will eat together anyway. Portia mentioned something about going on a youth group minigolf trip

with Mick, and my father still isn't up to joining us at the table."

"If he's at all open to having company I'd be happy to pay him a call while I'm there," Greg told her. He hadn't seen the older gentleman since he'd returned home from the hospital following his last health scare.

"That would be lovely," Winnie said. "We'll see you at one then."

Greg noticed that Miranda watched them both through this whole exchange with a questioning look. "So you're coming to lunch?" That told him this was Winnie's idea, but her niece didn't look unhappy about it, either. "At least that explains Aunt Winnie's floral arranging for an hour yesterday afternoon. And all the directions to Andre about those Chantilly cream puffs."

Winnie made a noise that sounded suspiciously like a giggle. "I do hope you like desserts, Reverend."

"Sweets are one of my weaknesses," he told her, wondering why Miranda blushed as they made their way out of the sanctuary and he greeted the family behind them.

"You could have warned me," Miranda told Winnie, trying not to sound like a huffy teenager. "I might have sounded more intelligent in front of Gregory if I'd known he was coming over for lunch."

"I don't think he's questioning your intelligence,

dear," Winnie said, patting her hand. "You could have said anything to him back there and he would still have thought you adorable."

"Aunt Winnie, really! This is your pastor you're talking about." Miranda felt her cheeks warm up even more. Could they get any redder than they'd been when Gregory smiled at her back there? She'd never felt so emotionally charged by a conversation about cream puffs before. "I can't imagine that the man thinks of me as anything more than one of the dozens of people he's counseled during hard times." She said the words firmly, trying to convince herself they were true. The kiss they'd shared had to have been an exception. Any attraction she felt for the handsome minister had to be one-sided, didn't it? What would a confident, educated man of God want with someone like her?

"If that's so, then he's done some very intense and interesting counseling. Nevertheless, he has to eat. And from what his secretary has told me during our quilting group, he's as hopeless as most bachelors about cooking anything more elaborate than hamburgers."

Miranda groaned. "You're matchmaking again, Aunt Winnie. Aren't you satisfied that all the rest of the girls have someone in their lives? With that many weddings and receptions to help plan eventually, surely you can let me be content in my spin-

sterhood." She said it as lightly as possible, hoping
to distract her aunt.

Winnie was difficult to distract and this time
wasn't any different. "Nonsense, dear. After all
these years of being a mother hen to that brood of
sisters you've helped me raise, you deserve better.
And in my estimation Pastor Greg might be the
only man in Stoneley worthy of your regard."

Miranda shook her head, knowing it was hopeless to argue with Winnie in one of these moods. "I
just hope you haven't told him that," she said,
cringing internally at the thought.

Winnie shook her head. "Of course not. Men need
to think these grand schemes are their own ideas."

"Is that why you've started leaving travel maga-
zines with articles about honeymoon world cruises
on the coffee tables every time Tate visits?" Finally,
something that deflected Winnie, who blushed even
deeper than Miranda felt her own cheeks redden.

"Why, I never…" was all Aunt Winnie could
splutter out. She stayed mercifully silent for the trip
home and Miranda filed that information away for
future use. There weren't too many ways to have the
last word with Winnie. It always helped to remember one that worked.

Once home, Miranda dithered about whether to
change her clothes or not. Gregory had said he would
be more casual than the dark suit he wore at church.
She had to admit to herself that the man would be

handsome in whatever he wore, even jeans and a sweatshirt. It was hard to picture him in that attire, given that she'd only seen him in what he called his work clothes so far. Thursday night he'd still worn a white shirt and tie when they went out for coffee. Remembering that, Miranda decided to stay in what she already wore. If she helped Winnie in the kitchen she'd put on an apron. Of course that would be if Andre let either of them in there today. He didn't always take well to Winnie's puttering around in there, especially not when company was coming.

Miranda felt very thankful that the day was nice enough to set the table on the sunporch for the meal. She counted places, coming up with eight. "Does this mean that Portia and Mick will be here?"

"And Kaitlyn. I thought with everyone present it would be safe to have your father and Tate at the same table. Surely the presence of the police, a small child and a minister will keep them apart."

"If that doesn't, Aunt Winnie, I have no idea what will." Miranda found herself sending up a small prayer that everyone's conduct would be up to Winnie's standards during Sunday dinner.

Mick and Kaitlyn arrived first, with Kaitlyn bouncing around in excitement after she'd given Portia a hug. "They're going to let me play minigolf with the youth group. I promised Daddy I wouldn't be too slow and make them wait."

"I just hope I can keep up with you myself,"

Portia said, drawing laughter from the group as she stood in the shelter of Mick's arms. Watching the comfortable relationship her sister and the tall detective had with each other, Miranda questioned whether she really could be as happy being single forever as she'd professed to Winnie earlier. Portia glowed with contentment, standing there with Mick's arms around her, both of them watching his daughter dance around in her bright T-shirt and denim skirt.

Winnie ushered Tate into the room, breaking into Miranda's thoughts. The older man and Mick greeted each other a little stiffly, but with more respect for each other than her father ever showed for Mr. Connolly. Tate welcomed hugs from Portia and Miranda with a look of bemusement on his face. "This family of yours takes some getting used to, Winnie," he said, gray eyes sparkling. "It seems like every time I'm around there are more of them."

"Don't you have any family, Mr. Connolly?" Kaitlyn piped up. "You look like a grandpa. Don't you have any grandkids?"

"No, miss, I don't," he told her, with a flicker of regret Miranda saw cross his face only briefly. "But I've got a nephew who's like a son to me, and I hope that someday his children will call me their grandpa."

"Well, if you want anybody to practice with, we can sit you next to Kaitlyn at the table," Portia said, smoothing one of the child's red pigtails.

"I might take you up on that. I'll never argue with having a beautiful redhead on either side of me for dinner," Tate quipped.

Kaitlyn grinned and Winnie blushed. It all made Miranda feel more surrounded by family than she had in quite a while. When the doorbell rang again she offered to get it.

Opening the door for Greg, she felt a little tongue-tied again. "I hope I'm not too late," he said. "It always takes longer to get home from church and change clothes than I expect it to on Sundays. I can't turn anyone away who needs to speak to me. Once I've been here just a little longer hopefully I'll be able to sort out who truly needs my time and who just wants company."

Knowing Greg's kindness the way she did, Miranda couldn't see him turning down even those who only needed a little visit. "So is this your disguise for going out in public to remain unnoticed?" Miranda couldn't help teasing him a little. He did look different in the pleated khakis and tan golf shirt he wore; more relaxed but no less handsome than he looked in a suit.

"I don't know about being unnoticed, but at least I'm not quite as visible to every member of Unity when I go out places like this. I hope it won't confuse your grandfather if I go upstairs to visit him dressed this way."

His genuine concern reflected on his face, and

Miranda felt touched by it. "Grandfather is so
easily confused on some days that I don't think
what you wear will have any bearing on what he
thinks, Gregory. I know he'll sense your kindness
and concern and that will mean more than what
you're wearing."

A trace of worry left his dark eyes. "That's nice
of you to say. I try to treat everyone the right way
no matter how I'm dressed. I think attitude is as
much a statement about Who you belong to as is
how you dress. It may be even more important,
because if I lack the proper demeanor the suit isn't
going to impress anybody."

"Well said as usual. Did you always have this
way with words or did you learn it as you studied
for the ministry?"

Greg smiled. "That depends on who you ask.
My roommates at the seminary would say I still
don't have their talent in turning a phrase, because
they're both married and I'm still single. I usually
respond that they are just fortunate to have found
young women right away who needed help curing
their insomnia."

Miranda laughed as she led him toward the living
room. "They must be good friends if they put up
with that."

The worry or unease was back in Greg's expression for a second, then gone. "The best. It's like
having a couple of brothers, only better. Dan and

Steve have never gotten into a fistfight with me."
Then they were in the large arched doorway of the
living room and Miranda made introductions, pon-
dering what Greg had said.

In a few minutes they all sat at the table on
Winnie's sunporch, trying to ignore the empty place
set for Ronald. "I'm sure he'll join us eventually,"
Winnie said.

Miranda knew the effort her aunt had put into
making sure dinner was just right, and she couldn't
help being aggravated that her father showed his
disrespect for his sister in this way. But then, why
should today be any different? Ronald didn't respect
much of anybody or anything, except his father and
the empire they'd built.

"If you'll say the blessing, Pastor Greg, I don't
believe we'll wait any longer for Ronald," Winnie
said tartly a few moments later.

Greg nodded and folded his hands in prayer, then
Kaitlyn broke in. "At home we hold hands with
each other. Can we do that here?"

"Of course," Greg told her, taking Winnie's hand
on one side of him at the circular table and Miranda's on the other. His touch started warmth
coursing through her, and she didn't even mind
having to stretch over her father's empty place to
reach Portia's soft hand. "Heavenly Father, thank
You for this beautiful day You have given us, and
for the good companionship at this table," he

prayed. "Thank You for this food, which I ask You to use to strengthen our bodies for Your service in whatever You would have us do. We ask this in the name of Jesus. Amen."

Miranda noticed that even Tate answered with an "amen" of his own, and she heard one from the doorway connecting the sunporch to the house. Ronald stood there looking a little sheepish. "I lost track of the time at the driving range, Winnie. I hope you'll forgive me for not being here at the start of things."

The explanation was so unlike her father's usual brush-off in such situations that Miranda felt taken aback. Perhaps God truly was working in her father's life. If that was the case, maybe there was hope for her as well.

Her brother's response surprised Winnie as well. "You made it in time for lunch, and from what I heard there behind me you were here for at least some of our table grace as well. I suppose we could overlook your tardiness this time. After all, I didn't call you three times, did I?" Her smile pointed out the dimple in her cheek. "It's something I'd almost forgotten from our childhood," she explained. "Our mother always claimed that Ronald was always so interested in playing with his friends that he never came in for meals until she called the third time."

Ronald slipped into place between his daughters. "My sister is right. But surely I at least have the sympathy from the other men at the table. I know you played a lot of football in your day, Connolly. Surely you two younger men came in late for dinner once in a while."

"Basketball at Jimmy McPherson's house," Mick put in, with more of a pleasant look on his face than Miranda had ever seen around her father before.

"Riding my bike down to the local park," Greg admitted. "Good to see you again, Mr. Blanchard." He extended a hand and the two of them shook in front of Miranda.

"That sounds like a subtle reminder that I haven't been to church with the family lately. And I suspect I might be the only one at this table who can say that."

"No, Ronald, you and I actually have something in common for a change, although I don't intend for us to have that in common long," Tate spoke up. "In fact, Reverend, I've been meaning to ask you what I'd need to do to join that church of yours that Winnie is so fond of."

Connolly's statement brought a hum of excitement to the table, and Miranda realized, along with the rest of the women, that this could only mean Tate and her aunt were getting closer to setting a wedding date. Light conversation about Unity and the programs they had to offer took up most of the conversation for a while. Miranda hardly noticed what she was eating because she was so absorbed in watching Gregory talk about programs for seniors and singles.

Only when Winnie brought out the cream puffs and coffee did Miranda pay attention to the entire table for a few minutes. Kaitlyn was trying to talk her father into staying "just a little while longer" so that she could have one of the concoctions. When Mick couldn't be swayed, Winnie came to the little girl's rescue. "I'll put three of them aside right now, dear. That way when you and your daddy bring Portia home after the youth group excursion, they'll be waiting for you, all right?"

"Thank you," Kaitlyn said. "If you marry Mr. Tate, maybe you can give him grandpa lessons, because you've sure got the spoiling kids thing down."

Her father only rolled his eyes, while Miranda knew she'd never seen Tate laugh so hard. When she looked over to her father, he seemed to have a wistful look in his eyes. Did he ever regret keeping so much distance from his daughters? Perhaps he could start over with grandchildren like Kaitlyn and the others who Miranda was sure would follow.

"Are you having one of these?" Greg asked, breaking into her deep thoughts. "They're fantastic, but then you probably know that already."

"It's not something we have very often," she told him, taking a small cream puff off the serving plate. "And I can't very well let you sit here alone and have your dessert, can I?"

"I planned to join him, Miranda," Tate told her.

"If I have one, we can probably even talk Winnie into sitting back down and enjoying dessert as well."

"Then while you do that, I'll walk down with these three and be on my way," Ronald said, rising quickly. "I hate to be the last here and one of the first to leave, but I have a golf game set up at the club in twenty minutes."

Naturally, Miranda thought. Her father could only sustain his best behavior so long. But no one argued and within a few minutes half the table had left.

"I still want to visit your father before I leave," Greg told Winnie over coffee. "Would it be best if you went with me?"

Winnie shook her head. "Actually Miranda would be a better companion if you're going to see Father. He's always doted on her and her sisters, and even now when he's so ill, he usually has a smile for his granddaughters. I only seem to upset him much of the time."

"All right, then. Once we finish here I hope you'll take me to see your grandfather, Miranda."

"Of course," she said. Another chance to be alone, if even for a moment, with Greg. She thought of showing him her studio while they were on the third floor. Then she remembered the eerie singing of last week. Visiting her grandfather would be plenty.

NINE

Every time Greg went through the Blanchard house he wanted to ask the inhabitants how they lived there. The place looked like a museum: marble floors, crystal chandeliers, artwork on the walls that probably exceeded his yearly salary by a factor of ten, and a lot of furniture he'd be afraid to sit on.

At least Winnie's sunporch had been a different story. All the way over here he'd been nervous about accepting her invitation, afraid that he'd be faced with elaborate place settings in the formal dining room and pick up the wrong fork in front of Ronald Blanchard. In his heart he knew that impressing any human being didn't have to be high on his list of priorities, but sometimes his brain had other ideas.

Now he'd survived the meal and Miranda was leading him to her grandfather's rooms. The front staircase and hallways leading from Winnie's sunporch to the old gentleman's part of the mansion were decorated in the style he usually associated with this place. Miranda, walking beside him, took all this luxury for granted. Seeing that made little doubts creep in about whether she could possibly ever be the woman that God had in mind for him.

Of course, after three meetings—two of them in the company of other people—and one kiss, he told himself he shouldn't be considering that anyway. Surely when the right woman came into his life he would know without a doubt…wouldn't he? Greg kept asking God that question but so far a firm answer eluded him.

When they reached the six-panel walnut door that led to her grandfather's rooms, Miranda stiffened. "This isn't right."

Greg couldn't see anything out of the ordinary. "What isn't right? All I see is an open door."

"That's it. Even when the private-duty nurses take over for Nurse Peg on her day off, the door is shut," she said, a furrow forming on her lovely forehead. She pushed the door even more widely open and Greg could hear raised voices coming from the room beyond.

"I don't want strangers accosting me in my home, young woman. If you want something from Blanchard Fabrics, come to my office on Monday morning!" The male voice was querulous and a little wheezy; it must have been Miranda's grandfather.

"Mr. Blanchard, I'm not a stranger. It's Alannah. You remember me, I'm sure," a smooth feminine voice replied. She appeared to think that volume would cut through the old gentleman's confusion.

"I've never seen you before in my life," Mr. Blanchard said. "Now get out of here before I call the police."

Miranda pushed past Greg. He followed her into the room as quickly as possible. "That won't be necessary, Grandfather. I'll make sure this person doesn't bother you again." Greg was seeing a side of Miranda he hadn't witnessed before. While normally she hung back a little, the possibility of a threat to her grandfather pushed her into action.

"Let me help you," he offered, firmly grasping the left arm of the wide-eyed redhead while Miranda took her right. "I'm sure Ms. Stafford doesn't want to disturb you, Mr. Blanchard."

"I don't know who you are, either, young fellow, but if you're helping Miranda out you must be okay." Howard Blanchard sat back in his armchair. "Come back when you're through, won't you, Miranda?"

"Of course we will. It won't be long." Miranda's voice was soothing until she crossed the threshold of her grandfather's suite. Then it hardened. "Now, Ms. Stafford, suppose you explain what on earth you were doing here as we go downstairs. Perhaps if you're pleasant we won't inform Detective Campbell and ask that you be charged with trespassing and assault."

Alannah tossed her finely cut hair. While the woman might have extremely poor judgment, she was impeccably dressed. Greg had to guess that her cream knit pants and top represented enough money to pay all of Unity's musicians for a Sunday morning. "You're kidding, right? I didn't assault anyone. And how can it possibly be trespassing when I have my own key?"

Miranda's glare told Greg that he didn't want to cross her anytime soon. The woman he'd figured for sweet-natured and calm didn't look that way now. She looked more like a protective mama bear. "If you have a key to any part of this house it's only because you didn't give it back when my father told you to. I believe that's still trespassing."

"You can believe whatever you like." They stood in the marble front hall and Alannah shook off their hands. "I just wanted to talk to Howard. He's always had a soft spot for me and I thought he could bring Ronald to his senses."

Miranda's lip curled. "My father came to his senses weeks ago and broke off the relationship he had with you. Using a man as ill as my grandfather to try to change that is reprehensible."

"If I'd had any idea how sick he was I wouldn't have tried it. Honestly, he's gone downhill severely in a very short time. How you keep him here is beyond me."

Miranda opened her mouth to speak, but before she could say anything Greg heard someone behind them. A small blond woman in a pale green top and pants pounded down the stairs. "What is going on here? Mr. Blanchard is terribly upset. I'm glad that I came back to check up on things."

"I have to admit, Peg, that if you had been here I doubt Ms. Stafford would have gotten into Grandfather's room." Miranda turned toward Greg. "Peg Henderson is my grandfather's nurse. She's taken care of him like a family member for the five years she's been in the house. Peg, I'd like you to meet Reverend Brown."

"I'll be happy to greet you in a few minutes, Reverend, as soon as we get *this person* out of the house." The petite woman headed toward the much taller Alannah, who backed away from her with both hands raised, palms out.

"I'm going. You don't have to come any closer. I'll be happy to leave on my own." Another toss of her head was probably designed to show off Alannah's expertly tinted and styled hair. Instead it made Greg think of a high-strung mare about to jump a fence. "This is the weirdest house I've ever been in. The entire place gives me the creeps."

"Perhaps that was guilt at being where you shouldn't have been," Greg told her.

"No, I think it was the security cameras in the powder room."

"Don't be ridiculous, Ms. Stafford. There's no such thing here." Miranda edged their unwelcome guest toward the front door.

"Right. I just *felt* someone was watching me the entire time I was in there. Just my imagination."

"Have it your way," Miranda said. "We will be watching you from now on, you can be sure. And I'll take that key." She held out her hand without saying another word.

At first Alannah merely pouted, but then she reached into a pocket and dropped the key into Miranda's outstretched palm as if she were getting rid of something distasteful. "Go ahead. I won't need it anymore."

Miranda's slim fingers closed over the key. "Good. If you want to contact my father I suggest you plan to do so through an attorney." She walked to the front door and pointedly held it open for Alannah. To emphasize the move, Greg stayed with the two women, herding the intruder toward the door.

Alannah looked at the two of them and glared, standing at the bottom of the stairs to the front portico of the house. "You're going to be so very, very sorry. All of you." Then she whirled and flounced out to the circular driveway. With hardly a backward glance she slid into a flashy black convertible and fled, tires spitting fine white rock as she took a corner a little too fast.

"Good riddance," said Peg so firmly Greg expected her to dust off her hands in the universal gesture of getting rid of someone. During the confrontation with Alannah, Greg had almost forgotten the nurse stood at the bottom of the stairs. "Now I'll go upstairs to your poor, dear grandfather. Perhaps after you give me a few minutes to calm him down the two of you could come up so that the Reverend and I can be formally introduced."

"I'll do that." Miranda looked at her watch. "We'll be up in fifteen minutes."

Peg nodded and went up the staircase almost as swiftly as she had come down. Miranda watched her leave with a heavy sigh. "You probably think we're hopeless, Gregory. All this money and prestige and we can't even protect one sick old man."

She called him Gregory. Where had that come from? Nobody had called him that since his mother died. From Miranda he liked it, though. She looked troubled, and Greg put a reassuring hand on her shoulder. "I don't think anyone could have foreseen something like this. Why don't you sit down for a few minutes and calm yourself. Do you think there's anything we need to do to alert the security staff about Ms. Stafford?"

Miranda went into the living room just off the hall and sat on a love seat. "I don't know. We've got the key now, so she can't get back in unless she made a duplicate. Given that it's her I wouldn't put that past her, so maybe I ought to call and leave a message for the security firm."

"And as you told Ms. Stafford, you ought to tell Mick right away, too. With everything that's happened to your family, he'd want to hear about something like this."

"That's true. Thank you for helping me."

Greg laughed. "What kind of guy would I be if I didn't protect a lady?"

"Definitely not the kind I've gotten to know that you are so far," Miranda said, eyes sparkling. The look of devotion she gave him made his stomach sink.

He wanted to tell her to back off. Falling for him would only lead her to be hurt. He wasn't the hero she seemed to think he was. And the last thing Miranda needed in her life was more pain. "How about we go up and visit your grandfather now," he suggested, trying to defuse the situation. Perhaps if he tried to just stay in his pastoral role they'd both be better off.

Miranda led Greg back to her grandfather's suite. This time the door was firmly shut as she expected it should be. That eased her mind a little, because it promised that Peg had put things in order again. She knocked and, after a moment, Peg came to the door. "Do come in, Miranda. I think he's much calmer now."

Peg motioned to the high-backed chair that was Howard's favorite. He sat there, looking considerably less upset than he had earlier with Alannah in the room. "Miranda's back and she brought that nice young man with her." She took Howard's hand

and Miranda was struck once more by how good Peg was with the older man. "Howard, this is Reverend Brown. He's the new pastor at Unity where Winnie goes to church."

"Good to meet you, young fellow. The way you backed Miranda up back there I thought you might be part of the security staff."

"No, just coming to make a call on you, actually. I thought you might want a chance to hear the Good News and perhaps have me pray with you." Gregory took Howard's hand and shook it gently, then sat in the chair closest to him to put Miranda's grandfather at ease.

Miranda marveled at how quickly he connected with Howard. Given that her grandfather was notoriously hard to make friends with at this time of his life, the visit really played up Greg's talent.

Howard gave a dry laugh that almost turned into a wheeze. Peg hovered over him and he waved her away. "I'm all right, Peg. She worries about me like a mother hen," he said. "And I don't want your prayers, Reverend Brown. The Good News left this house for me when my Ethel died."

Miranda felt a twist of sorrow listening to her grandfather. He lived in the past more and more these days, and his past hadn't been a happy place for a long time.

"I'm sorry you feel that way, sir. I believe that Jesus is always here to walk beside us in our troubles, even the worst of them. Scripture tells us that He is a man of sorrows. There's no place of pain that we can be in where He hasn't been there first. No place of joy, either, but that's a different story," Greg said.

"That it truly is, and one I'm not nearly as familiar with, I'm afraid." For a moment Howard looked thoughtful in a way Miranda hadn't seen in quite some time.

"Why don't you tell me a little bit about Ethel," Greg suggested, leaning forward in his chair.

Howard brightened and began to hold forth. Miranda sat quietly and listened to more than she'd ever heard about the grandmother who had died long before she was born.

If her grandfather's remembrances were right about his wife, Miranda mused about how different all of their lives might have been had she lived. With a woman that strong and loving by his side, would Howard have taken such an instant dislike to Mama? And without that stress in her life, would her mother have gone down the path she did, leading to her disappearance?

Greg put in an occasional word, drawing more out of Howard. The old man's eyes blazed and he gestured with his hands, enjoying his own story. "And let me tell you, young man, Ethel was beautiful on the outside, not just the inside. She was tall and dark haired and absolutely stunning. Not at all like my—"

"Howard, you've worn yourself out," Peg cut in sharply, breaking off what he was saying.

Miranda felt dismay. For a moment she was all set to hear her grandfather say something about her mother. Instead he looked up at Peg and nodded.

"Yes, I imagine you're right." Howard settled back in his chair. "Perhaps I ought to take a nap."

"It's my fault," Greg said, looking at Peg apologetically. "I've overstayed my time listening to Mr. Blanchard's story." He stood and Miranda joined him. "If you'll indulge me I'll say a very short prayer."

Greg put a hand gently on Howard's shoulder. Peg opened her mouth to say something but must have thought better of it, because she stayed silent. Miranda, bowing her head, was surprised to see out of the corner of her eye how perturbed her grandfather's nurse looked.

"Dear Lord, thank you for the gift of the long marriage to Ethel that you gave to Howard. You know the pain he feels in his heart from missing her, and the hardships of illness and age that he bears as well. Please find ways to remind him how much You love him. Thank You for the kind care You have brought him in the ministry of Peg and the love of his family. We pray in Your name, as You taught us," he said, and began the familiar words of the Lord's Prayer. Even Howard joined in, surprising Miranda.

When they had finished Greg said a quick good-bye to Howard and Peg. Then Miranda led him back out of her grandfather's suite. "That was really something in there. I've never heard that much about my grandmother before."

"Have you asked?" Greg's brown eyes searched her face.

"I have, but I don't think the timing was ever right. Listening to Grandfather really makes me wonder how different everything would have been in our family if my grandmother had lived."

Greg took her hands and she could feel a rush of warmth through her. "It's hard to know what might have been. And it's almost never helpful, because all that we can do is second-guess life."

The depth of feeling in his words made Miranda wonder what kind of second-guessing he might have done about his own life. Before she could ask, the moment passed and he let go of her hands.

"I've probably overstayed my welcome with more than your grandfather." He made a wry face. "I need to head home and see what's on my agenda for tomorrow, I guess."

Miranda wanted to protest, to keep him for much longer, but that wasn't her place. Gregory was responsible to a few hundred people as senior pastor of Unity. She couldn't keep him around just for her comfort. Reluctantly she went down the stairs with him. When they got to the first floor they went looking for Winnie. She didn't seem to be inside, and when Miranda noticed the sunshine outdoors, she knew where her aunt was likely to be.

She took Gregory out to the rose garden. Winnie, changed into her gardening clothes and floppy hat, stood between two large bushes taking dead blooms off them. "So, how was your visit with Father?" she asked. Miranda could tell from her expression that her aunt felt a bit anxious about things.

"It was interesting," Greg replied. "I tried to calm him down a little after the incident with Ms. Stafford, but I'm not sure I didn't make things worse."

"Ms. Stafford? Do you mean to say that she was in this house?" Miranda thought Alannah should feel thankful that Winnie, brandishing her garden shears, hadn't been the one to find her.

"She was, but not for long," she told Winnie. "And we got back the key she used to get in."

"Good," Winnie said. "I can't say I was ever fond of Ms. Stafford. She always seemed to walk around here as if she were appraising the furniture."

Greg laughed, a sound Miranda found charming. It was an honest, open laugh, gathering delight from what Winnie said, even though her words might not be the kindest thing for a Christian to say. Before Miranda could add anything to the discussion, another voice said, "Okay, let me in on the joke."

Some of the fun went out of things when she

realized it was Ronald, coming home with his golf clubs after his foursome dropped out. Even in golf clothes he looked stiff and formal.

"We were just discussing Alannah Stafford," Winnie said, waving her shears for emphasis. "Who, I might add, paid us an unscheduled visit this afternoon."

"When I went to call on your father, Ms. Stafford was in his room talking to him," Greg said to Ronald, whose expression darkened immediately.

"How did that happen? I can't imagine anyone letting her in."

"She had a key, Father. But we got it back and Pastor Greg helped escort her to the door." Around her father, Miranda felt like referring to Greg in more formal terms.

"Was Mick still here? If he was, I hope you had him help evict her."

"Mick and Portia left just after you did," Greg told him. "They were hosting a youth group event this afternoon. I suggested notifying the police about Ms. Stafford."

"Good. They should be notified. Even if she doesn't have a key anymore, she's dangerous. She made some pretty bold threats to me and my family when I broke off our relationship."

"And she made another one today. Before she left, she told us that everyone was going to be terribly sorry. Do you have a cell-phone number for

Portia or Mick?" Greg was looking directly at her, his dark eyes troubled.

"Inside, somewhere in my room or studio I do. Is this urgent enough to call them before they get back from their outing?" Miranda felt a shiver up her spine.

"I'd say so. Before I leave, promise me you'll tell Mick all about this, and file a police report if he thinks it's necessary."

"Of course. Do you think he'll really want that?" Miranda felt a great deal of confusion. She had tried all afternoon to convince herself that he didn't care for her in any personal way, but this action muddied the waters.

"He had better," Ronald said. "That woman is not to be trusted. I still don't regret breaking off my relationship with her, but I do wish I'd had the foresight to make more provisions for my family's protection."

"Hindsight is always a great thing," Greg said. "At least you can feel fortunate that you have a couple of police officers as future sons-in-law."

Ronald's answering smile seemed a little weak. Miranda thought about how Mick and Drew intimidated her father. She decided to put an end to the conversation to avoid further embarrassment. "Why don't you let me walk you to your car? I know you still have work to do." She reached out a hand to Greg and started walking to the front of the house where his car was parked.

Greg nodded. They covered the distance in

silence, with Greg letting go of her hand when they reached the end of the grass at the driveway. "Tell your aunt thank you for a nice lunch."

"I will. I'm just sorry things got a little strange afterward."

Greg shook his head. "Don't worry about it. I was happy to help with Ms. Stafford. Most of the time when someone needs my services, it has a lot more to do with my pastoral skills than with muscle." He struck a brief "strong man" pose and smiled. "I don't usually get to be the tough guy. I kind of enjoyed it."

He said little more before driving off, and Miranda found herself watching his car pull away as she wondered what exactly was happening between her and the handsome young minister.

TEN

Journal entry
June 12

I can't stand it anymore. Ronald wants nothing to do with me, thanks to his daughters and that awful woman. He's never going to change his mind so there's only one thing to do. At least my darling Ronald will be beyond suspicion again now.

Normally when Greg came back from lunch, the only person waiting in the outer office was Janice. And that was if they hadn't had lunch together. Once or twice a week the two of them went out for a quick meal together at the Lighthouse Café or somewhere else they could be served speedily and get back to the office. They used the time to discuss church business without as much stress as they'd have in the office. Slowly but surely Greg was working his way through the pictorial directory of the membership, memorizing names and faces, family relationships, and all the information that Janice had and he needed.

Today, though, Mick Campbell and another man Greg wasn't sure he recognized sat waiting in the chairs near Janice. When he came through the door, all three of them looked at him intensely. Mick sprang up and held out his hand even as Greg extended his.

"Hi, Mick. What's up?"

"Some fairly serious stuff." Mick looked more somber than usual, and Greg wondered if someone else from the congregation had gotten themselves in some sort of trouble the police detective wanted to discuss. "Can we go into your office?" He motioned to the closed door.

"Sure." Greg got out his keys and unlocked the door, ushering the men through.

"This is my partner, Drew Lancaster." The other man, who still hadn't spoken, nodded. Somehow Greg would have suspected he was in law enforcement even if he hadn't been next to Mick.

"Pleased to meet you, I think. I have to assume there's trouble somewhere if you're both here. Would you like to sit down and tell me what's on your minds?"

Greg sat in his desk chair and the other men grabbed the visitors' chairs. Neither of them relaxed in their seats. Communication passed between the two in a brief glance and Drew cleared his throat. "I understand you were at the Blanchards' home on Sunday. A police report that Mr. Blanchard and his daughter Miranda filed stated that you helped escort Alannah Stafford off the property. Is that correct?"

Where was this going? Greg wasn't quite sure, but he had no problem answering truthfully. "I helped with that, but not in any physical sense except taking Ms. Stafford's arm at one point. I hope she hasn't complained about her treatment."

"Not exactly." Drew's dark eyes gave little away. "Did you hear her issue any threats to you or the family?"

"She told us that everyone would be 'very sorry' but she didn't go into any detail. At the time I wasn't sure whether her statement was a threat or a promise." Had the lovely socialite gotten herself a lawyer? From what little he'd seen of her, Greg thought it was highly likely.

"How upset did Ms. Stafford seem as she left the house on Sunday? Upset enough to do harm to anyone?"

Now Greg felt uneasy. Had she gone back and done something to anyone there? If so, Miranda could be a prime target for her wrath. "Ms. Stafford was angry. Did Miranda or her father tell you that before we removed her from the property, Miranda confiscated a key to the house that had been in Alannah's possession?"

"She mentioned it." Mick didn't look pleased. "I took the report myself, after Portia and I got back Sunday afternoon, and I wondered out loud how Ms. Stafford got into the house. That's when they told me about the key, which meant we couldn't charge her with breaking and entering."

"I know you probably won't be able to tell me much, but is everyone okay at the Blanchard house? I'm concerned that your coming here and asking these questions might mean that Ms. Stafford hurt someone."

The silence that answered Greg made him even more uncomfortable. Finally Mick sighed and looked at his partner. "We can tell him that much," he said.

Drew raised one shoulder in a half shrug. "It's not exactly policy, but you trust him and that's good enough for me."

"None of the Blanchards have been harmed. We received an anonymous tip yesterday that implicated Ms. Stafford in a serious crime. When we tried to reach her to set up a time to discuss what the caller had said, we didn't have any luck. A visit to her condo complex showed her car in its stall in the parking garage, and none of the neighbors remembered seeing her for a couple days."

Everything Mick said rang alarm bells for Greg. Now some of Alannah's actions Sunday took on a new meaning. Telling everybody they'd be sorry for their actions, coupled with her assurance that she wouldn't need a key to Ronald's house anymore led him to one uneasy conclusion.

"You know, in retrospect, several things she said that last time I saw her take on a different meaning when I think about them," Greg said. "In my work as a pastoral counselor when someone tells people that they'll be sorry because of what they did to them, it can mean trouble."

Mick nodded. "Yes, that can be a threat or a promise all too often. But you said several things?"

"The other big one was how easily Alannah gave back that key, when I would have expected her to put up a fight to keep it. Somebody who starts giving things that they value away without protest may be thinking about suicide. It's one of the warning signs."

Drew's eyes widened and he looked at Greg as if he suddenly had more respect for him. "You're pretty good at this. But then when I think about it, some of your counseling work must be a lot like ours, uncovering clues about someone's life."

Greg felt his shoulders slump. "I'm glad Ms. Stafford didn't harm anyone else, but this must mean she took her own life."

Mick nodded. "Everything we found inside her condo seems to point to that."

Greg knew the man well enough to sense what he wasn't saying. "You don't sound totally convinced about that."

"I'm not. All the evidence we found suggests that she committed suicide, and a journal and note near the body provide plenty of explanation. But she was shot, and I would have figured that anybody as concerned as Ms. Stafford seemed to be with appearances would have done something that didn't risk disfigurement. We'll know more in a few days when the medical examiner makes his initial report."

Drew stood and his partner followed. "Thank you for your time, Reverend Brown. If we have any other questions, can we find you here?"

"All too often," Greg told him, thinking as he said it that he needed to call Miranda soon to see how she was doing. "Has the Blanchard family been told of this yet?"

"As soon as we could after notifying Ms. Stafford's family. By tomorrow the media's going to be all over this anyway, probably sensationalizing it as they go."

Great. Now there would be another round of media attention for Miranda and her family. He needed to make that call as quickly as possible.

Friday morning Miranda and Winnie had breakfast in Winnie's sitting room, as they had for several days. "They're still there," Winnie said, looking out the window. "I thought perhaps we were done with the vultures for a while."

"Now you know that something as dramatic as a

suicide like this one would draw the media back again," Miranda said, suppressing a shiver. She didn't feel any more charitable toward the men and women who camped out in front of the house with cameras and satellite trucks, hoping to talk with Ronald or someone in the family or on the staff. So far they'd been unsuccessful as far as she could see. "I wonder where they're getting their information."

Winnie sat down at the table, looking piqued. "Not from anyone here, that's for certain. And Mick is sure there've been no leaks through the police department. Personally I think it might be someone in the medical examiner's office. I've known most of the county commissioners for at least twenty years, and I don't think many of the employees are paid enough. Some low-level employee probably saw the chance to make a little money and didn't consider the consequences."

Winnie looked pointedly at the local newspaper, folded discreetly so that the current day's headline about Alannah was obscured. Miranda had already read the story, though, and knew its sordid contents. "I didn't ever care for Alannah, but it was because of the way she clung to Father, obviously out for his money. I never thought her capable of something like all of this."

"Quite honestly, I didn't either. But she seems to have confessed to murder and attempted murder as well." Winnie's hazel eyes, normally so bright, looked sorrowful today. Miranda knew her aunt ached for the pain Alannah must have kept to herself. "If she truly did these things, I don't understand how she could have gone on this long without going to the police."

"We may never know more than we do now," Miranda murmured, thinking again how desperate someone had to be to take their own life. "Still, Mick says that the gun she…left behind on the floor…is definitely the same one that Genie was shot with." Miranda couldn't bring herself to say out loud that Alannah had killed herself, just as she wasn't ready to call the other woman who had been killed "Aunt Genie." The actions of both poor, misguided souls disturbed her a great deal. Even if the media hadn't been parked outside the front door, she wasn't too sure that she would have made it outside in the past few days.

Just thinking about it all, Miranda could feel her muscles tense and her breathing become a little ragged. "Are you all right, dear?" Winnie asked a bit sharply. "Perhaps we shouldn't discuss this if it's upsetting you."

"I don't know." Miranda sighed. "I think I need to talk about it, but I don't know how."

Winnie seemed to make a decision, and she smiled as she poured herself a fragrant cup of Earl Grey tea. "Then I'm glad that I phoned the church this morning."

"Why is that?" Miranda had an idea she knew what would be coming, and she wasn't sure whether to thank her aunt or cause a very unlady-like scene instead.

"I thought we could both use a little help and advice from our pastor." Winnie's smile was a little fainter now, but it still played around the corners of her mouth. "I hope you won't object. Pastor Greg seemed to be such a help to you on other occasions."

"He has been, but I hate to take him away from his other work at Unity. I'm sure he has a dozen more important things to do."

"On the contrary, he almost jumped at the chance to come out here. I think he had been waiting for the call."

"He offered when we spoke yesterday, but I told him then it probably wasn't necessary," Miranda admitted. "But I think I'm glad you called him, Aunt. He was so helpful when Alannah was here, and honestly, I could use someone to talk to."

"A strong shoulder to lean on always comes in handy," Winnie said, not bothering to hide her smile now at all. "I think Tate will be over for lunch as well. He's been insisting that I let him come over, and if anybody I know could scatter that mob outside, it would be Tate Connelly."

Miranda reached for a slice of toast from the rack. Her aunt probably had other jobs for Tate besides dispersing the media, but she didn't feel like teasing Winnie today. After all, she'd had the courage to call Gregory and have him come out when Miranda couldn't do it for herself, no matter how much she wanted to.

Before noon most of the crowd outside had been dispersed, and Tate and Gregory stood in the front hall talking more comfortably than Miranda would have dreamed possible. But then, both men were used to being leaders in their own way, and had no lack of communication skills.

"You can congratulate me all you like, Reverend, but I have a feeling that my skill in handling the media wasn't what made them all leave. I suspect it had much more to do with the fact that we told them about that press conference at Blanchard Fabrics." Tate shook his head. "Although I can't imagine, Winnie, what that brother of yours is paying his law firm to get the charges against him dropped this quickly."

"Now, Mr. Connelly, I'm sure any good firm could make the argument that with a signed confession from someone else regarding the crime Mr. Blanchard was charged with…"

"Even though she's conveniently unable to explain more," Tate said, his lip curling.

"Still, there is a confession, and the police reports appear to confirm that the same person wrote the note and the journal found near Ms. Stafford's body. With that in mind, it's logical that Mr. Blanchard's lawyers could get the charges against him dropped."

"Winnie, as much as I love you, I believe your brother is getting off easy this time. The police may not be disputing anything at this point, but I just don't like this whole situation."

"No one likes it, Tate. Now let's go upstairs and have lunch. Perhaps we can talk about more pleasant subjects for the first half hour or so, like how one plans a tasteful wedding service for a bride whose hair will be as white as her dress."

"Now, Winnie, you're exaggerating," Tate said, putting his arm around her protectively.

Miranda found herself smiling as she watched her aunt and Tate start up the stairs together. Even though many terrible things had happened to her family lately, this newfound happiness for Winnie was a blessing everyone could share.

"I get a kick out of those two. I don't know all their history, but she seems to have made quite a change in his life by becoming a part of it again." Greg's words reminded Miranda that there were whole layers of her family history that this man didn't know.

They started up the stairs, a flight behind Tate and Winnie. "I'm not sure I know it all myself, but I do know that any good that comes Winnie's way is something she deserves. She's been the only real parent that my sisters and I have had since our mother disappeared." She sighed. "My father was too wrapped up in his bitterness and his business to have any time for us. Winnie kept my mother's memory alive, tried to pass on her own strong faith to us all, and just loved us in every way possible."

"From what she says, you had a lot to do with raising your sisters, too." Greg's eyes appeared moist for a moment, but that passed quickly. "That had to be a heavy burden for a girl not yet into her teens."

"I was the oldest. Juliet was an infant with no memory of our mother, and truly, all the girls except Bianca and me were very young. I did what I could. I think most of it was to keep my mother's memory alive for myself." It was the first time Miranda had admitted that to anybody else, and it felt freeing somehow.

"Being a child growing up in this house can't have been easy." Greg's expression invited Miranda to say more, and around him talking came easier than with anyone else she'd known in years. "I'm glad you had Winnie."

"So am I. And I'm glad she introduced me to you." Miranda felt like blushing the minute she said that, but Greg's answering smile gave the warmth rushing to her face a different sensation.

"I'm glad, too." He took her hand, and his tenderness overwhelmed her. "Now how about we catch up with those two and see if we can start planning a wedding. Honestly, I'd rather do just about anything to keep from discussing your father and his legal situation with Mr. Connolly anymore."

"I couldn't agree with you more. I think Winnie's biggest problem is who to have stand up for her as a witness. Tate has his nephew, Brandon, but I don't think Winnie wants to pick just one of us."

"I expect we can work something out. From what I've seen of you and your sisters, I'm not about to stir up anything among this many strong women."

If Miranda hadn't felt love for him before, it swelled in her now. A few weeks ago, when Winnie told her that Gregory Brown might be the only man in Stoneley worth her time, she hadn't believed her. But now once again her aunt was proving to be a woman of great wisdom.

"Well, I heard she just couldn't live with herself after killing the wrong woman. She thought she was setting herself up to be the second Mrs. Blanchard and she totally blew it." Greg didn't recognize the young woman gossiping about Alannah Stafford, or the well-dressed man she was talking to, but he was tempted to introduce himself just to startle them. This party at the Blanchard home reminded him of Winnie's birthday party back in January in its scope, but that was where the comparison ended.

Winnie's party had been filled with happiness for the most part. In January he was still getting used to Stoneley and its society and now, more than five months later, he had made many more contacts. Tonight's party felt totally different; Ronald Blanchard's assistant Barbara Sanchez had gone all out in planning the affair to celebrate charges against her boss being dropped. If it hadn't been for his wanting to see Miranda through what might be an uncomfortable evening, Greg would have stayed home and worked some more on Sunday's sermon, even though it was only Wednesday night.

Now perhaps he had even more grist for that sermon, especially since the text he'd chosen was the seventh chapter of Matthew that began with the warning that we would be judged as we judged others. Before Greg could give any more thought to the issue of judgment, he had other problems— trying to keep his balance while being almost bowled over by a bubbly Kaitlyn Campbell. "Hi, Pastor Greg. I'm staying up past my bedtime!"

"I can see that, young lady. What does your dad have to say about that?"

"That I have Portia's daddy to thank for that because this is his party. I haven't seen him yet to say thank you." She stood on tiptoe in her white summer sandals. "You're tall. Can you see him from up there?"

"Not yet. But I do see your dad and Portia," he told her, swinging her up off the ground as she giggled. He was glad that the brief trauma of being kidnapped hadn't scarred the child, and she was still the sweet young lady he'd come to know. Watching her father and Portia search the crowd for the child, he wondered how much Miranda's sister had sacrificed during the abduction to keep the child protected. Not for the first time he thanked God for His wisdom in putting his friend Mick in contact with this beautiful, strong woman.

As he lowered her to the floor, Kaitlyn wiggled down out of his grasp and raced to where her father stood. Greg followed her to have a few words with Mick and Portia. "This is quite a party," he said, not going into detail so that he wouldn't be forced to say anything he didn't mean.

"Not exactly my style," Portia said, wrinkling her pretty nose slightly. "I would have been happy with some kind of family dinner, but Barbara seemed to believe the entire town needed to be invited. And I think they all came." She gestured to the overflow crowd in the living room, the marble entrance foyer and the dining room, where the chairs had been removed around the massive table to give more space to circulate.

"I know I saw the mayor when I came in, and I think he was talking to your boss," Greg said, looking at Mick. "Is that how she got you to dress up this much?" Campbell didn't look too comfortable in the suit and tie he wore.

"Nah, I did it on my own. I figure dressed like this nobody would recognize me and I could circulate more freely, hear what people are saying."

Greg started to laugh, but realized the detective

was at least half serious. "Well, I won't keep you then. Enjoy the evening."

They parted and Greg slipped into the dining room, wondering where Miranda might be. He'd been looking for her, sure that any minute he'd see the cascade of dark, wavy hair that always tempted him to run his fingers through its masses, or catch the scent of her subtle, floral perfume. So far he had made a quick circuit through the living room, where Ronald was holding court with various business and city officials.

From there he'd looked through the dining room quickly, and then gone back to the entry hall where he'd seen the Campbells and Portia. Now he returned to the dining room, where he thought he recognized Miranda's sister Juliet and her fiancé Brandon DeWitt. He considered asking Juliet where Miranda was, then a server who looked like she might work for a caterer swung the door from a butler's pantry wide-open as she carried a tray to the table.

Beyond her in the kitchen Greg finally saw Miranda. Impulsively he headed toward her, even though he knew that going into the kitchen wasn't polite guest behavior during a party at someone else's home.

"Hi," he said, not wanting to startle Miranda with his presence.

She turned, and her answering smile spoke of anything but being startled. "Hello. I was hoping that you would be here. I spent the first hour or so among the guests, but everything out there was getting on my nerves. I thought perhaps I'd calm down if I came in here."

"Did it work?" She didn't look all that calm to Greg, but she certainly looked beautiful.

"Not terribly well. Do you have any other ideas on how to escape the crowd without being too rude?"

"Rude or not, why don't we take a walk along the bluffs. It's warm in here and there are too many people."

Miranda's answering smile was even wider than the first one. "That's brilliant. Let me tell someone where I'm going and I'll be right back."

"Hurry. Now that I found you I'm ready to escape."

ELEVEN

Walking along the bluffs with Greg, Miranda felt like a new person. Inside, the house had closed in on her until she saw Gregory. Now out here with the velvety sky full of stars and a light breeze teasing her hair the tension of the party seemed miles away.

"I'm glad you rescued me," she said, squeezing Greg's hand. He'd taken hers the moment they'd left the path. Miranda wasn't sure whether he was protecting her from falling, or letting her guide him through unfamiliar territory. Either way, it was wonderful.

"I think we rescued each other. I can't say I was here for any reason but to see you," he told her, which made her heart flutter.

"Personally I think it's kind of a sad reason for a party. But I guess it figures with my father's image as the CEO of Blanchard Fabrics. And I imagine it gives his attorneys the publicity they want as well."

"But, as you said, all that adds up to a pretty pitiful reason for a party. I couldn't help comparing it to Winnie's birthday party. That was the last big event I attended in your family's home. Now there was a reason for celebration."

Even in the dark she could see and feel Greg's smile. "I felt the same way tonight before you came. Except for Grandfather's outburst with Alannah and Juliet in January, Aunt Winnie's party was so joyous. Tonight feels so…I don't know…hollow in comparison."

"For somebody who doesn't consider herself terribly spiritual, you certainly are rather deep. And we're often on the same track on things, like what you just said."

They had come to the weather-worn porch swing that had been on the bluffs here as long as Miranda could remember. "Well, if we're on the same track, then maybe you'd like a chance to sit down as much as I would," she said, trying to sound lighthearted.

"That would be fine. I didn't sit down much inside because there just wasn't a group I wanted to join in there."

She sank to the smooth gray seat of the swing in its frame, the chains holding the swing creaking softly. The salt air had worked on this swing for decades. Occasionally someone replaced it, but it always seemed to weather to this homey piece of furniture quickly. Greg sat down beside her, sighing contentedly. "This is very comfortable. Do you come here often?"

"It's one of my favorite places after Winnie's rose garden. Sometimes when I'm looking for inspiration that won't come, I walk out and sit here and stare out there at the ocean until the horizon blurs." It wasn't something she'd shared with many people; her family already counted her as the resident daydreamer and she didn't have many writing friends she would have trusted with something this private.

"Wow. That sounds positively poetic. In the nicest sense of the word, I mean." Greg relaxed back into the swing, setting it swaying softly with the push of his long legs. He reached above his head in a move that reminded Miranda of a teenager at the movies, draping an arm across the back of the swing.

It would feel so good, she thought, just to lean back onto that strong arm and stay there. Greg must have thought so, too, because he didn't move when she did settle in with a small, happy sigh. For a little while they just sat there together and Miranda looked up at the brightening stars.

"Can you teach someone to write poetry? I've always felt that it was sort of an inborn talent, somehow. I feel I'm miserable at it, personally. I look at the poetry of the psalms and it moves me, but I can't imagine writing it."

"You can teach some parts of writing anything, but I have to think there's something inborn as well. You can teach someone how to reach what's already there inside them, but you can't create that 'something' if it's not there."

"Wow. Can I take that idea for a sermon sometime? It's a very powerful idea."

Miranda sat up a little straighter. "You would use something I said in a sermon? I hardly feel worthy of that."

"None of us are worthy by ourselves. It's the Spirit working in us that brings that worthiness. And what you said about teaching someone to reach something inside, but not being able to create that something, is a very deep Christian idea. If we believe it's the grace of God that saves us through faith, we're talking about 'something' being there inside us that we can't create, because God's the One who put it there."

"And what I said led you to all of that? I'm impressed. I thought we were simply talking about writing poetry. And by the way, I think you might be better at that than you think." It was on the tip of her tongue to say that his eloquence around her was one of the things she loved about him, but something stopped her.

"I don't know about that—" Greg broke off what he was saying and looked down. In the silence Miranda could hear a faint hum and there seemed to be a glow coming from somewhere. "My cell phone." Greg sighed. "I have to at least see who's calling."

He fished the offending phone out of his pocket

and glanced at the display. "I have to take this one for just a minute." He flipped it open as he stood up from the swing and walked a couple of steps into the darkness. "Hello? Yes, I know, Aunt Martha, I didn't call this week."

So it was a family call. Miranda tried not to eavesdrop, but it was difficult. She wondered what Greg would tell his aunt about what he was doing right at the moment. "No, nothing is wrong. I've just been very busy. Mostly routine stuff, but there has been a bit of excitement, too."

Miranda's pulse raced. Had Greg said anything about her to his family yet? She wasn't familiar enough with the ways of men in general to know what to expect. In the faint light she could tell that Greg looked over to where she still sat. "Say hi for me," she said softly on impulse.

"What? Oh, Miranda says hi." There was a short pause. "No, she's just a friend who goes to Unity. I'm at a party her family is giving. It's a large celebration. I even ran into my best girl Kaitlyn earlier. That's right, the cute one with the red hair."

Miranda's heart sank to the pit of her stomach. So she was just a friend from church. And he mentioned her in the same breath as a six-year-old. *That's what you get for saying something,* she told herself bitterly. Now you *really* know what he thinks of you.

Hot tears threatened to spill over as she sat

staring at the ground, her hands balled into fists.
As usual she wasn't carrying a handkerchief or
tissues. A knot tightened her throat, but for a
change it didn't signal a panic attack coming on,
just a huge dose of hurt and disappointment. No
longer listening to Greg's conversation, she stood
up and started heading back to the house. Half-
blinded by tears she almost stumbled ten feet from
the swing, but steadied herself. She almost looked
back around to see if Greg had noticed. No sense
in that. He was too busy talking to someone he
really loved.

Greg almost hung up on Aunt Martha and Uncle
Vince when he turned and noticed the empty swing.
The moment he'd told his aunt that the soft voice
she'd heard in the background just belonged to a
friend, he knew he was in trouble. Still, how could
he explain to Miranda that his aunt was such a hopelessly romantic person, with a vivid imagination?

If he admitted that Miranda might be anything
more than a friend, Martha would mentally be planning the wedding already. No, Greg resolved years
ago not to talk about women with his aunt. The one
time he'd brought a girl home from college just
because she had nowhere to go on Thanksgiving
weekend, he'd come downstairs for Saturday breakfast to find Martha showing his poor, hapless friend
clippings and baby pictures from a scrapbook. After

that he'd always been very careful to err on the side of caution with Martha.

Greg knew his attention had left the conversation when he heard Vince call sharply, "Son? You still with us or has that space-age phone of yours run out of juice?" Vince didn't believe anybody needed a telephone that could fit in a pocket and contained a day planner, games and a digital camera.

"No, the phone's fine. I just need to get back to the party before they miss me," Greg said. No sense in telling them that what he really had to get back to was a young woman he needed to have a talk with. That alone would get Martha going. They said their goodbyes and Greg hurried up the path searching for Miranda.

"Hey, wait up. We need to talk," he told her as he caught sight of her in front of him, hurrying toward the well-lit kitchen.

Miranda stopped, but she didn't move toward him. "I think you've talked plenty." Even in the near-dark Greg could see tears glistening on her cheeks. He reached out toward her and she stepped back, palms out in a gesture that could only mean *stop*.

"Will you at least let me try to explain?" That sounded pretty lame even to him. "I know you heard me say you were just a friend, but there's more to it than what you heard."

Miranda dashed the back of her hand across her cheek. "There's more? Oh, great. Next you'll tell me it's not me, it's you. Any other lines you want to run by me?"

Greg stood there speechless. Was he being that shallow and transparent? Because he'd never been in this position before, he had absolutely no practice in what to do next. If Miranda would let him he would gather her into his arms and hold her and ask her to try to put up with his fumbling attempts to apologize and make things right. But she didn't want anything to do with him.

Of course, this just proved that she didn't need somebody like him to add more pain to her life. "No, there are no more lines, Miranda. But will you please stay here with me a moment so I can get my act together and say things right for a change?"

"No. If you have to think about it all that much, there's really nothing more to say." Leaving him in the dark, she turned and nearly ran back to the kitchen door. Greg stood there watching her disappear into the brightly lit house while he tried to figure out what on earth he should do next.

A few of the catering staff looked at him a bit oddly when he rushed through the kitchen on his mission to find Miranda. He didn't find her there, or in the dining room. When he scanned the crowd in the hall his heart sank when he saw a bevy of women just rounding the corner of the staircase to the second story of the house.

"All right, just what is going on here, Pastor Greg?"

Winnie's voice nearby made him start. "Miranda came in looking quite upset, talking in an animated fashion with Bianca and Portia. Then Bianca gathered the rest of her sisters from where they'd been around the house and they all trooped upstairs."

"What would happen if I followed them?" Greg watched the group disappear from view.

"You'd get a door slammed in your face at best. None of the 'menfolk' went up there. Apparently there's some kind of conference call set up with a new private investigator that Bianca has found. Even Delia is being patched in from Hawaii."

"Whoa. Serious stuff." He wondered if Miranda had known about that when she went outside with him. Had she been willing to give up an important meeting with her sisters just to be with him? If so, he was in even deeper trouble than he thought.

"Extremely serious stuff. I hope to hear what they learn this evening. I know that Bianca is praying for concrete proof of her mother's survival, and an idea of where Trudy might be. And the others are doing the same." Winnie's eyes held unshed tears.

"What do you think they'll find?" Greg discovered he was holding his breath waiting for the answer.

"What I hope and pray for is that they'll find Trudy alive and in as good a shape as is possible. Although I have no idea how well she might be after all those years in that place Bianca and Delia told me about. I try to convince myself that it's possible someone might find Trudy and find her relatively well." Her face softened into a small, hopeful smile. "After all, you're always reminding us that with God all things are possible."

"This is true. And tonight I need to be reminded of that myself. Thanks for providing the reminder." Just hearing the words, he felt a little more comfortable. He'd been trying to second-guess God for a while now, wondering if Miranda could possibly be the "right" person for him, and deciding that might not be possible. God, however, might have a totally different idea.

"I'm more than happy to return even a little of the inspiration you've given to me." Winnie patted his arm. "Now, how about we get away from this party a bit. I know you're a history buff. Would you like the historical tour of the house? I'll even tell you the truth behind all the gossip."

"Winnie, you're on. And if that tour might possibly end up on the second floor in about forty-five minutes, that wouldn't be a bad thing either."

She shook her head slightly. "I'll say one thing for you, Pastor Greg. You're determined."

Greg felt like telling her she had no idea how determined he could be once he put his mind to it.

There weren't a lot of secrets in the living room or dining room. The tour went through those quickly, skirting the groups of people surrounding Ronald in the living room and a small cluster of

Blanchard Fabrics management types who'd taken up residence in the dining room. The kitchen held more interest for Winnie, and even more interesting was the cellar entrance near it.

Winnie unlocked the door to the cellar and flipped on a light switch on the cold stone wall. "Now watch your step going down here. The stairs are old and wooden, but they're sturdy. If you have problems with cobwebs, we'll forget this part of the house."

"Cobwebs are okay. I'm not real keen on rodents, though." It cost Greg something to admit that, but it would have been even harder if Winnie saw his reaction should a rat slink out of a corner.

"Me neither. As long as I live in this house, you can be assured there won't be mice or rats inside the property." She shuddered slightly. "I can't argue with them outside, but in here is my territory."

Reassured, Greg followed Winnie down the stairs to the cellar. It proved to be relatively well lit and very clean, though there was an air of dampness about it. "This close to the ocean, I'm surprised the water table allows for a basement," he said, wondering how it was possible.

"We have a very good sump pump," Winnie said. "There's also another little secret." Crossing the space to the far wall, she motioned to a doorway. The heavy oak door had several locks. "Through there is a secret passage. It leads down to a second level, so if water does rise to that level, it stays there."

"Does the secret passage go anywhere?"

"Of course. It wouldn't be worth the name otherwise, would it? It's actually more of a room than a passage, but at the other end it connects to the caves that are down at beach level."

"Caves?" Greg's interest level rose. "Have you ever explored them?"

"Once years ago. I discovered that I liked bats even less than I liked mice, and I spent most of my time in the caves worrying that they might house thousands of the little creatures."

"I can appreciate that. Do the caves have history connected to them?"

'Naturally. There are still barrels and crates down there from when they were used by smugglers over two hundred years ago. And during Prohibition I'm told that gangsters from Boston used them as a way station for illegal alcohol."

"Sounds like there would be plenty to explore, then. Do you think Miranda might be interested?"

Winnie laughed softly. "I thought this discussion might be headed in that direction. And actually, yes, it's possible that she would like to explore the caves. Of course you would want to do some work mapping them out first yourself, or go to the Stoneley Historical society and see what they have there regarding the caves. I would insist on that, just to be sure the two of you would be safe."

"Why? Are there dangers other than the occasional bat?" Maybe the caves were unstable. In that case he wouldn't take Miranda down there.

"Not really dangers, just situations to be aware of. As I remember the lowest of the caves floods at high tide, so you wouldn't be able to get in or out that way very safely. Otherwise, there's not much I can think of that would be a problem."

"Great. I don't mind having an excuse to spend some time at the Historical Society." Especially, Greg thought, when it might result in a way to patch things up with Miranda.

"Would you like to see the back staircase up to the second and third floors, and the more public parts of the second floor as well? I'd offer to show you my library, but I believe that's where the girls are taking their conference call."

"I would love to see as much of the house as you'll show me," Greg told her. "And I'll make special note of your library for future reference." Not all that far in the future, either. He planned to be directly outside that library door when Miranda came out.

When the door to Winnie's library finally opened, Miranda and Bianca were the first ones out. Bianca had one arm around her sister and was talking in an animated fashion. "You just have to say something to him, Miranda. If he doesn't respond with an apology, then you'll know…" She trailed off when she saw Greg in the hallway.

"Well, Reverend Brown. Your timing couldn't be more perfect." She turned to Miranda and gave her a brief hug. "Okay, you're on your own now. I need to rescue Leo before Father bores him to tears." She gave Greg a smile that didn't seem to reach her eyes and left.

"I wasn't trying to eavesdrop," Greg told her. "Your aunt gave me a tour of the house and I made her show me where her library was."

"And you knew we were inside?" Miranda's gaze challenged him.

"I did. And I decided that even if it took another hour of standing here and looking rather foolish, I'd wait for you to come out." It gave him a lift to watch her small, shy smile.

"Lucky for you, our new private investigator is to the point."

"Did he give you good news?" Greg didn't see anything on Miranda's face that would indicate more unhappiness since she'd gone upstairs.

"*She* was rather encouraging. Cat says she can trace Mama as far as her family beach house in California. Some of the evidence there indicates that she might have been there as late as early April."

"That's great, Miranda. If I packed a beach picnic and showed up on your doorstep tomorrow afternoon about one o'clock, would you tell me more? I promise I'll guard my tongue so I don't make any more blunders."

Miranda stood there with a quizzical look while Greg prayed silently that she would say yes.

"All right," she finally said. "I imagine that a beach picnic is appropriate for friends."

"More than appropriate. And I want to talk about developing our friendship into something deeper." Greg knew his voice trembled a little over the last statement, but so be it. Where Miranda was concerned a little anxiety was worth it if it gave him a second chance.

TWELVE

"Stop pacing the hall, Miranda. You're going to wear out the marble." Bianca sat on the grand staircase in the front hall in fashionable jeans and a cotton T-shirt, grinning while she watched her sister complete another circuit of the entryway.

"Oh, dry up." Miranda did stop pacing, but not to please her sister. "You have no idea how nervous I am."

"Because of a picnic? Come on."

"Because of who invited me on the picnic, and I said yes!" Her voice rose on the last word. Miranda knew it made her sound a little panicked, but that was the way she felt. "You were there right behind me. Why didn't you stop me?"

"You're a big girl. Nobody wrung an answer out of you. If you didn't want to go on the picnic all you had to do was say no. Since you didn't turn Greg down, he is probably right in believing that you want to see him again."

"I do… I think," Miranda admitted tersely. "But I have no idea what to say and I'm sure I'm going to make an even bigger fool of myself than I did last night."

Bianca shook her head. "Judging from what you told us before we talked to Cat, I'm not sure that's possible."

Miranda gave up pacing altogether and came to sit down next to her sister. Bianca might be only a year younger, but she'd always been more worldly-wise. "You think I should have confronted him last night?"

Bianca tilted her head. "Yes, I do. And you also have to realize that hearing a man tell someone else that you're 'just a friend' is a bit different from having him tell *you* that he just wants to be friends."

Miranda tried not to moan. "Wasn't that going to be the next step?"

"Not necessarily. Did you even give him a chance to explain himself?"

"No. I was so sure of what I was going to hear that I told him not to say anything else. Not too bright, huh?" She felt like burying her head in her hands and having a good cry.

"I don't know about whether it was bright or not, but it was certainly a normal response." Bianca put an arm around her and Miranda was conscious of the beautiful diamond ring on her sister's left hand. Leo Santiago had extremely good taste in jewelry.

"Do you want to pray about it? We could while we wait, you know."

"Sure." Miranda leaned her head down to touch Bianca's. "Dear Lord, please help me. I don't know what to say or do when Gregory comes for our picnic. I know he's a good man, and that he loves You. Help me to see him as You see him, as a beloved child of God. In Jesus' name we pray." Her sister added little more, and they sat in silence for a few minutes.

"You really do care about him, don't you?" Bianca said softly. "After seeing him last night, I can see why, and unless I've become a poorer judge of character than I used to be, I think the good pastor wants to be more than just friends with you, sis."

Miranda felt her eyes fill with tears. "Oh, I hope so. But what do I do…" The ring of the front doorbell cut off her thoughts. When she crossed the expanse of tile to open the door, there stood Greg wearing a pale blue polo shirt, khakis, and carrying an elaborate picnic basket.

"Hi. I hope I'm not too late. I have to admit that I went to Gourmet to Go and picked up lunch. I didn't want to inflict my cooking on you yet." His boyish smile was so charming that Miranda found herself smiling back.

"No, you're right on time," she said, ushering him into the hallway. "Come in and say hi to my sister Bianca before she leaves."

Bianca's eyes glittered with delight as she greeted Greg. When she took off up the stairs after a few minutes, she got to the first landing and made a circled-finger "okay" sign and winked at Miranda, who felt like throwing a shoe at her. But then, she had to admit, Bianca's gesture had relaxed her.

"So, do you have a favorite spot for picnics?" Greg asked, twenty minutes later when they made it to the beach.

"It varies, depending on the weather and the kind of mood I'm in. If I'm happy it's usually down here on the beach where I can watch the sandpipers run around. Something about them makes me laugh."

"And if you're not as happy?" Greg asked casually, but he seemed to be paying a lot of attention to her answer.

"Then probably up on the bluff, either at the old swing where we were last night or at a bench a little farther down. The bench is one that Grandfather put there especially for Grandmother Ethel. It makes me feel a little melancholy to sit there, wondering what she was like."

"Did she leave any journals or anything like that?"

Miranda shook her head. "Just a few photographs and a family Bible that Aunt Winnie keeps in her library. She had beautiful handwriting."

"So, which spot is it to be today? I hope you'll tell me that we stay on the beach." A light breeze blew through Greg's sandy-brown hair, picking out highlights of gold Miranda hadn't noticed before. For someone who spent most of his time inside, he seemed to be in his element out here.

"Definitely the beach," she told him. "That's why I brought along a second bag. I keep an old blanket in it just for such occasions."

"Great. I'll let you pick the spot. You can probably find us the right place on a beautiful day like this." They walked along for a little while as Miranda listened to the rush of waves and the cries of the seabirds.

"Right here," she said, pointing. From the spot she chose they could see the entrance to the caves that led below the house. Putting down the basket, he helped her spread out the blanket. Down here on the shore with the breeze blowing, Miranda was glad she'd tied a cotton sweater around her waist when they set out. Her long chambray skirt and the T-shirt she wore had felt great when they set out from the house, but here it felt five to ten degrees cooler than it had been in the rose garden.

"So, what prompted you to ask me on a beach picnic?" Miranda asked Greg, half an hour later when they were finishing up the sandwiches he'd produced from his well-packed picnic basket.

"Several things. I didn't want to ask you out in case you were having a difficult day." The understanding in his eyes touched her heart.

"I appreciate that. I haven't had as many of

those difficult days lately. Some of that may be due to you."

"Now why do you say that? There've been plenty of people who have helped you get to this point. I suspect your aunt has had more to do with your lack of difficult days than I might."

"I think the thing I owe most to my aunt right now is that she introduced me to you." Miranda hadn't intended to say that, but somehow she couldn't keep much from Greg. "Her faith has always been a good example for me, and I know she's prayed for me every day for more than twenty years. So even in things like her ever-present match-making she has the best in mind."

"She definitely seems to. I guess I should feel honored that she believes I'm worthy of you."

From anyone else Miranda would have felt that she was being teased, but Greg's expression was one of sincerity.

"I'm the one who ought to wonder about worthiness. I understand there must be a dozen reasons why being any more than just friends would be a bad idea," Miranda said.

"Funny, right now I can't think of any." Greg took her hand and Miranda felt warmth course through her. The breeze might still be blowing but it didn't bother her now. "I know I said that before, but it came out all wrong, Miranda. I wasn't trying to push you away. It's just that there's so much about me you don't know. So much nobody in Stoneley knows and I've been happy to keep things that way."

"Gregory, I can't imagine that there's anything about you that would be half as bad as some of the things the media has reported about the Blanchard family just in the time you've been at Unity. You're just too kind and caring and honest for me to believe anything else."

He looked down at the picnic blanket and Miranda wanted to reach out with her free hand and touch his face, bring his gaze back to hers. But somehow the gesture felt too intimate and she resisted the impulse. "Then you'd be surprised. But you have to believe me when I tell you that it's nothing about you that has made me hold back from being anything but your friend. I've already seen the amount of pain the world has thrown at you in the last six months. You don't need any more."

"Doesn't the Bible say that we're not supposed to judge other people? I don't think it's fair to either of us for you to try to figure out what I can or can't handle. I think you should leave the decision up to me."

Greg's brown eyes widened. "You know, that's a very good point. I've been trying to protect you from several things when I should have just told you and let you decide where to go from there."

"Or we could decide together. That seems fairest

to me." Was it her imagination, or did his grasp of her hand tighten?

"That sounds like a great idea. And if we're trying to be fair here, would it be fair to ask you if it's okay if I kiss you?" His hand was definitely tighter.

"Yes. It would be fair. And yes, I'd like it if you kissed me." Miranda didn't even close her eyes in anticipation. This time she wanted to savor every bit of Gregory's kiss with all of her senses including sight. And this time it was very, very good.

She came to him with her eyes wide-open. Greg thought he'd never seen anything braver. He'd just told Miranda that he wasn't the person up on a pedestal that she'd created and she didn't seem to care. She met him right where he was, in the moment, and she did it without reservation. In that gesture he received the message that wiped away the doubt he'd felt before. He had been telling himself that surely the woman God had in mind for him as a life partner would be all the things a church expected a pastor's wife to be. That way he'd erected a barrier that kept him holding Miranda—and anybody else he might have judged unworthy—at arm's length.

Now Miranda had found a way through the barrier. She couldn't have found that way by herself; God had to be leading the charge. This all had to be something from God, because it had His fingerprints all over it. Here was this person right in front of him, coming to him unafraid and seeing everything, willing to love him just where he was and just as he was. *Does this remind you of anyone you already know?* a small voice inside of him teased. Of course it did. The risen Lord that he spent every day trying to serve worked exactly the same way.

Greg realized, in the time he had taken to come to grips with all of this, he had kept the kiss going with Miranda. Drawing back reluctantly, he sat there on the blanket with her, feeling breathless and a little stunned. "Wow," was all he could say for quite some time.

As if there was an echo mixing in with the crash of waves on the nearby shore, Miranda mirrored his comment. "Wow is right. I'm thirty-three years old and, obviously, I've been kissed before. Or at least I thought I had been. After that, though, I'd have to say that I've been kissed before but I haven't really been *kissed* until just now."

She was going to think he was a real idiot, but all Greg could do was nod as he sat listening to the waves and holding Miranda's hand. For a few moments the touch and the silence was enough. Finally he had to break the spell. "Do you think I should take you back to the house?" he asked.

"I do," she answered. Miranda looked as solemn, in a thoughtful kind of way, as Greg felt. Together they slowly packed up the remains of the picnic, folded the beach blanket and started for the house at the top of the bluffs.

"It feels so good to be out here in the fresh air," Greg said, enjoying the salt tang of the air and the breeze that ruffled Miranda's long skirt. "Maybe we can do something else together outside soon. Winnie gave me an idea for another outing that you might like."

"Oh? Tell me more." Miranda looked over her shoulder and smiled at him. Her smile picked him up every time he saw it, which wasn't enough for his taste. "Where we ate lunch down there wasn't too far from the entrance to some caves she told me about during the tour of the house she gave me. Have you ever been in them?"

Miranda shook her head. "Not really. I've been in the part of the cellar that leads to them, but that's as far as I ever went. And naturally that was with Delia and Juliet egging me on when we were all much younger."

"I want to really get to know your sister Delia sometime. What little I've seen, and everything I've heard, makes me think that she must be quite an interesting woman."

Miranda laughed. "All my sisters are interesting women. What I wouldn't give to have all six of us sit down with Mama and ask her where we get some of the traits that I certainly don't see as part of the Blanchard legacy. I talked to my grandmother

Eleanor when she was here but somehow it just isn't the same."

Greg couldn't resist coming closer and gathering her in his arms to try to ease the wistful look on her face. "I hope and pray that someday soon you'll get the chance to ask her, Miranda. If your mother is alive, it's difficult for me to imagine a situation where God wouldn't let that happen."

"And thanks to Cat, our new private investigator, we're all surer than ever that she's alive, or at least she was recently." She leaned her head on his shoulder and Greg had to fight not to hug her too tightly. Miranda brought out a strong urge in him to protect her, but he had to let her be strong and independent, too.

"There you two are," a cheery voice called out, making Miranda stand up straight again. Winnie, wearing a floppy straw hat and a denim dress came toward them with rose-pruning shears in hand. "Greg, could we induce you to stay a while longer than you'd planned this afternoon? I know you must be busy, but it's such a glorious day that I'm trying to do something spur of the moment."

"And what would that be, Winnie? Coming from you, that could mean something quite interesting."

"Just tea in the gazebo, mostly family. Almost all of the girls voiced their opinion that last night's party was a little over-the-top, and I thought perhaps we could enjoy the roses at their height and one another's company at the same time. It's getting to be a rare occasion when this many of them are home." Winnie's brow wrinkled slightly. "And I suppose it will be even rarer as more of them marry. But then, that's the way God intends things, isn't it?"

"'A man will leave his mother and father and join with his wife and they become one,'" Greg said in agreement, quoting Matthew. "And since you seem to be instrumental in a lot of these prospective 'joinings' then you have to accept them."

"Yes, but I certainly hope most of them settle near here so that I can play with their children," Winnie said.

Greg was about to laugh, but noticed that Miranda was flushing bright pink, so he tried not to do anything that might embarrass her further.

"So, back to tea in the gazebo," Greg said, redirecting the conversation a bit. "Will Mr. Blanchard be joining us?"

Winnie sniffed. "The only Blanchard male joining us will be my father, Pastor Greg. Ronald is back to work, business as usual. But it's such a beautiful day that Peg agreed to have Father come down on the elevator so he might enjoy the sunshine."

"In that case I'd be happy to stay," he told Winnie. Even though it probably meant he'd be in his office late tonight once he got back to the church, it would be worth it to really get to know Miranda's family better.

"I think you impressed Winnie with your willingness to move furniture and help set up everything," Miranda told him about ninety minutes later when everything was all arranged in the gazebo and Sonja and one of her helpers were busy setting the tea tables.

"Hey, you'd be surprised at how many food-service jobs I can do. It comes from working my way through college and seminary," Greg told her. "You should see me clean a kitchen."

"You're probably much better at it than I am," she said, smiling.

"Better at what?" Juliet asked as she bounced up the steps to the gazebo. She hugged Miranda quickly on the fly then came over to Greg.

"Good afternoon, Juliet. I'm surprised your father gave you the day off to visit with your sisters."

She shook her head, laughing. "I've got so much comp time coming that I could take off a week already. I even convinced Brandon that he should use some of his and quit early so that he could join us."

The young woman glowed with health, and her happiness when she mentioned Brandon DeWitt made her even more beautiful. "You certainly look better than the last time we really got a chance to talk."

Juliet wrinkled her nose. "Nobody looks good after being poisoned. Do you think Alannah put Marc up to that?" she asked, referring to the chef's assistant who had been planted in the Blanchard household for malicious purposes. "I'll confess to reading the newspaper articles about her journal, and it makes me wonder…"

"Don't believe everything you read, kid." Mick Campbell strode up behind his future sister-in-law and patted her on the head about the same way he might Kaitlyn. Juliet grimaced at him but otherwise let the gesture pass. As the oldest and youngest members of this family group, Greg suspected that they must have their share of run-ins.

Before any more of a fracas could start, Winnie was there directing traffic and instructing the men present on how to position a ramp up the two stairs to the gazebo so that Howard and his wheelchair could join them with ease. It was a good twenty minutes before everyone settled down again and by then other topics of conversation had come up.

Greg looked at the plate in front of him, wondering if he'd ever get used to the kind of household where a woman like Winnie could decide in the morning to have tea in the rose garden and have this array of sandwiches, pastries and cookies at her fingertips by afternoon. Tate Connolly seemed to be wondering the same sort of thing. He caught Greg's eye and shrugged, smiling. It wasn't his style, but obviously almost anything Winnie did met with his approval.

Miranda stood up and the group quieted around their round tables spread through the gazebo. "Before I forget, I've got a question. Who's been inside the caves under the house? Gregory wants us to go explore them and I want to make sure it's all right."

"You're getting my sister in those caves? I'm impressed," Juliet said. "The farthest we could ever get her was the passageway from the basement. Even though we assured her they were perfectly safe as long as you avoid high tide, she wouldn't ever go in."

"What happens at high tide?" Brandon asked from beside her.

Greg knew the answer to that one. "The entrance from the beach floods and you can't see where the sharp spots are on the cave floor. And in some places it gets deep enough that anyone but a strong swimmer would be in trouble."

"Now how did you know that?" Mick asked.

"I made a trip to the Historical Society archives," Greg admitted. "They've got great maps of the place."

"What are they talking about?" Howard Blanchard seemed to stir from the doze he'd been in since Peg Henderson had wheeled him into the gazebo.

"Caves, Grandfather. The ones that join to the house." Portia, sitting close to him, spoke loudly enough for him to understand.

"Caves? Never liked them myself. But I heard something about them not too long ago. What was it, Peg?"

"I think it was on the television, Howard. You know how you like those nature shows." She smiled at him indulgently. "Now that you're awake, do you want a cookie? Andre made those cinnamon ones you're so fond of."

Greg wondered what it must be like to come to the end of a long life like Howard Blanchard's and be faced with all the decisions one had made over the course of eighty plus years. What did he regret? What was he proud of? Looking at Miranda standing beside him, Greg decided that if he got that old, she was the kind of woman he'd want by his side.

Catching his eye, it was as if Miranda somehow understood some part of his thoughts. Sitting down swiftly, she continued to look deeply into his eyes. He took her hand and they sat quietly as the swells of conversation rose around them.

THIRTEEN

"So, are you ready for this?" Greg stood outside the back door, wearing jeans, hiking boots and a sweatshirt over a button-down shirt. "I want to make sure that you're dressed right for this. Have you ever done any serious hiking before?"

"Not really." Miranda looked down at her outfit. "I borrowed something from everybody, I think. Juliet insisted I take a pair of her old jeans, Winnie gave me a sweater and Portia made sure I had waterproof shoes. She's so petite I can't wear anything of hers, but she knows just what to wear for almost anything."

"I love it. You've been dressed by committee. And they did a good job of it, too. All I might recommend is a hat."

Miranda felt herself blushing. "I've actually got one, but it's so out of my usual realm that I left it in my room. Mick left a Police Association ball cap here and Portia insisted I take it. I've never worn a ball cap in my entire life."

"I bet you'd look cute in it, though. But then I'm beginning to believe you might look cute in just about anything."

He was actually flirting with her! Miranda found herself grinning. Maybe with Greg she might even learn to flirt back.

"Come on in and let's get this going," she said. "The first thing I want to do is go down into the basement and make sure that the door there is unlocked. I don't want to go into the cave that way. It would feel like cheating. But if we stay in there past high tide in a couple hours, I want to make sure we have a way out."

"Good thinking. It sounds like between us we might have this covered."

For the first time Miranda noticed the backpack Greg carried. "Does this mean you've got supplies in there?"

"Just the basics. Sometimes I break the cardinal rule of most outdoor activity and hike alone. I know you're not supposed to do that, but some weeks my hike on Monday or Tuesday is my only real alone time." He shrugged. "Janice worries when I do that, so I try to reassure her by carrying this. In it is my cell phone, a couple bottles of water, a flashlight, rope and a very small first-aid kit. All that is probably overkill for a cave that's directly under your house, but I thought it might reassure you."

"It does." She'd known Greg was a clearheaded

kind of guy, and now she had proof. Any lingering doubt she'd had about this excursion evaporated. By now they were in the basement facing the heavy door that led into the cellar passageway. Miranda took a set of keys from a hook near the door and unlocked both locks. She tried the knob and, after a little work, the heavy door swung inward, letting in a blast of cold, dank air. "At least we have proof that we can get through that way," she said.

Leaving the lights on, they went upstairs. Greg followed along while Miranda got her cap. "Maybe afterward I'll show you my studio," she told him as they went down the back stairs to the first floor. With Gregory beside her that incident of hearing eerie music several weeks ago felt half a lifetime away.

Outside in the sunshine it felt ever further away. It didn't take long to get down to the beach and stand before the entrance to the cave. Miranda took a deep breath. "Well, let's do it."

"In a moment. I think we should say a prayer together first." Greg faced her and took her hands in his. How did the man keep such warm hands all the time? "Lord, thank You for this wonderful day. Please keep us safe on this adventure together, and show us the wonders of this small part of Your world. Guide us in the direction You would have us go. We ask all this in Jesus' name."

"Amen," Miranda said. What had prompted Greg to add that part about guidance? She didn't know whether to ask him about it or not, so she stayed quiet. Greg took two flashlights out of his pack and they went into the cave.

For a while the path was fairly wide, and the size of the entrance let in a fair amount of light. "I can see why it would be dangerous at high tide." Miranda played her flashlight over the uneven floor. In some places there was smooth rock, but in others sand and piles of beach shale made navigating more difficult. Twice as they went a little farther back into the cave, Greg had to help her step over little rivulets of water. In the half-light it was impossible to tell whether the streams were a few feet deep or bottomless.

After a while the passage narrowed to about seven feet across. "I can imagine smugglers using this for a hideout, can't you?" Greg motioned with his flashlight down a passage branching off from the main way. "The maps at the Historical Society show at least half-a-dozen places that could have been used as storerooms."

Miranda shivered, glad now that she had Winnie's sweater on over her shirt. The deeper they went, the cooler and moister the air in the cave. "Do you think any of the little splashing noises might be rats?"

"It could be," Greg said. "But I think it's more likely just dripping water someplace, or maybe a pool back here somewhere that's deep enough for small fish or some frogs. Even rats need some day-light part of the time."

He squeezed her hand and Miranda squeezed back, glad that he hadn't let her go after fording the last little wet spot. Some men might have laughed at her fear, but Greg had simply calmly reassured her instead.

The passageway sloped downward a little and widened into a room. In the light of Greg's larger flashlight Miranda could see a few crates stacked in a far corner, and several barrels in another. "Probably leftovers from our rum-running friends," Greg said. "I wonder if we're looking at evidence of pirates or bootleggers."

"Either way, it's good to think that for a change there's proof of something nefarious going on in Stoneley that didn't involve my family. Even Grandfather would have been too young during Prohibition to be involved with anything down here."

"True," Greg agreed. "Although I imagine the old gentleman might have a few stories if we asked him. You know, many people with Alzheimer's have less trouble relating an incident from their youth than telling you what they did yesterday."

Miranda wondered what Howard might have to say about the caves and their possible contents. Had the cellar been built the way it was on purpose, to access the smugglers' caves? Perhaps for a change she could have a conversation with her grandfather that might leave him in a better mood than she found him. The thought made her smile.

Somewhere ahead Miranda heard a small, liquid-sounding *plop*. Training her flashlight on the area she thought the sound came from, she didn't see a frog or anything more threatening, but something caught the light and glittered.

"I want to see what's over there," she told Greg, pointing the beam of her light. They crossed the broad expanse, and Miranda stumbled a little several times while trying to avoid small pools of water. Once something made the surface beneath them slippery, and she almost fell.

"Maybe you might be better off over there." Greg motioned to where a stone outcropping made what looked like a low bench coming out of the side of the cave wall. Miranda nodded and splashed over to the spot.

"Do you see anything else?" she asked a few minutes later when Greg reached the spot where she'd seen something that caught her eye.

"I do, but I'm not sure how to make sense of it all. I'll bring it over to you and maybe with the two lights together it will be clearer." Greg shifted his light to his left hand and picked up two small objects with his right. Picking his way carefully to where Miranda sat, he put his treasures down beside her.

"Are you sure you don't have kids from town sneaking around here to party?" Greg's expression looked fairly serious. "Although there aren't any cans strewn around, and no evidence that anyone has made a fire." He seemed to be deep in thought about something, and Miranda looked at the objects he'd laid down.

In the shared beam of their flashlights Miranda saw a syringe and needle, and a discarded pill bottle. Now she could see why Greg looked worried. Stoneley was small enough that most people felt safe here. If there was some kind of heavy drug trade going on around them, they would feel far less safe.

"Wait a minute." Miranda picked up the orange plastic bottle. Reading the label stunned her. "This is one of Grandfather's prescriptions. How on earth did it get down here? And why? Was there anything else strange where you found the bottle and the needle?"

"Not right there. But go over with me. I want to use both lights to search that niche in the wall."

Greg led her carefully across the uneven cave floor and directed her where to shine her light. "There. Do you see it?" On a ledge about five feet up something shone in the beams of light. He slid into the small chamber and reached up on the ledge. Taking the object down, he examined it. "It's a necklace. Looks like a locket."

He handed it to Miranda, who felt cold spread through her as she examined the small piece of jewelry in her hand. The heavy twisted gold chain held a filigreed locket with a clasp. Stunned, she handed her flashlight to Gregory. "Hold this and aim it on the locket. My hands are shaking and I want to see what's inside."

Taking the flashlight, Greg did as she asked. Trembling, she made three attempts at opening the locket before she succeeded. "There's something written there."

"'To thine own self be true,'" Miranda said, almost in a whisper.

"How can you tell in this poor light?"

"I've seen it before." Miranda wasn't sure how much longer her knees would let her stand. "I learned how to read script by tracing this. It's my mother's locket, Gregory. The one she never took off."

Greg was afraid he was going to have to drop the flashlights and catch Miranda. Her wide eyes and wavering voice made him fear she was going to pass out on him. She steadied herself against the damp cave wall with one hand. "She's alive," she said slowly. "She has to be. The only reason Mama would have taken this off was to leave somebody a message. To leave *us* a message. It has to mean that she's been here recently."

"Are you sure?" Even as Greg asked it, he knew what Miranda would say.

"I'm as sure of this as I've been about anything in a long time." Her eyes were full of tears when she looked up at him. "We have got to get back to the house. If Mama has been this close, and she's no longer in these caves, then she has to be on the estate somewhere."

"Let's go." Greg put his arm around Miranda and guided her toward the back of the cave, where they hadn't been yet. He prayed it would be an easy journey. Most of the cave floor felt smoother toward the back of the space, and after a short stretch the narrower passage opened up into a fair-size room. "We'll come back and explore all of this another time." Greg gestured toward the stacks of crates and the barrels near a doorway cut into the stone and framed with ancient-looking wood.

They went through the doorway and crossed into the chamber that Greg figured was the one that led into the Blanchard cellar. This looked more like a room or a storehouse, with the stairs Miranda had described yesterday leading up three steps to a landing built of heavy planks. "Come on, Miranda. We'll get to the bottom of this."

"I hope so." Miranda stopped in her tracks. "Gregory! I just realized something. That night I told you about, in my studio. Maybe I wasn't just imagining I heard music. Maybe it was Mama, trying to get a message to me. If so she's been in the house for weeks!"

"Then we had better hurry." Greg turned to lead Miranda across the floor and up the stairs.

"That's as far as you're going," a cold voice said

from the landing. The light from the doorway behind the figure made Greg strain to see who it was. He knew he'd heard that voice before, but somehow it sounded different. Today it sounded more detached and more in control than before.

"Peg? Is something wrong with Grandfather?" Miranda hurried toward the blond woman Greg now recognized. In her hurry Miranda pulled away from him, and in the dark she must have hit a damp patch of floor and slipped. Pitching forward with a cry, she fell before Greg could catch her.

"Nothing's wrong with the old man yet. But give it an hour and he'll be gone."

"What are you talking about?" Miranda asked before Greg could. He couldn't understand what Howard's nurse meant, or why she suddenly sounded so stern.

"My darling wants him gone. He says the old man has become a nuisance and it's time for him to go. I think he finally realizes we're meant to be together. And you certainly aren't going to get in our way."

In the time Greg had taken to stoop and help Miranda to her feet, a gun had materialized in Peg's hand, and it was pointed at Miranda. "You can't mean that," he said as calmly as possible. If this woman was as disturbed as she sounded and holding a loaded gun, he couldn't take a chance on aggravating her.

"Oh, I mean it. I've been waiting for the sign that

I needed to take action, and yesterday you gave it to me." Peg pointed the gun in Greg's direction and he took the opportunity to step slightly in front of Miranda so that he could protect her.

Greg tried to understand what Peg was telling them. What "sign" had he given her that pushed her over the edge? "Ah. You mean that Miranda and I planned to explore the caves," he said, and was rewarded by a gleam in her eyes.

"Of course. Once you were down here it was only a matter of time before everyone knew that stupid woman was alive. I was pretty sure that Genie hadn't covered her tracks well enough, but I couldn't find time to get down here and clean things up. The one time I tried to leave Howard alone that long, it led to even more disaster." She scowled in disgust. "Leave him in someone else's care for thirty minutes and that vain Alannah gets to him. After that I couldn't very well leave him until I got rid of her."

"Got rid of her? You mean she didn't commit suicide?" Miranda sounded stunned, and Greg could feel her shivering under his touch. If only Peg would drop her guard for a moment so he could move in.

"No, she didn't commit suicide," Peg said, mocking Miranda's tone perfectly. "But I fooled everyone into thinking she did. No one ever questioned whether that journal was hers, or the validity of the confession I left for the police to find. And Alannah was so easy to kill. She let me in without question once I called her and told her I knew how she could get back into Ronald's good graces. As if I'd ever do that."

So many little things were falling into place. Greg wasn't sure what bothered him more—the way this evil woman's mind worked, or the fact that he understood her. "You really *were* watching her when she came here to see Howard, weren't you? That's why she complained about feeling she was under surveillance."

"It wasn't what I'd planned to do. She just chose the wrong place at the wrong time. She was always so nosy. Some people just ruin everything." The statement seemed to bring Peg back into the present, and Greg's heart sank when she took aim on him with the gun again. He had no doubt that it was loaded and that she could use it.

"And I've come too far for anybody to ruin things now. Once I'm free, and Ronald is free, everything will just fall into place. I'm too close to that happening to let you come between us now." She motioned with the gun toward Miranda. "Now step back from this door. Farther. If either of you comes any closer I'll shoot Miranda."

The woman might be deranged, but she still knew how to manipulate him, Greg thought. Somehow they had to get out of this without Miranda being harmed. For now he pretended to obey Peg to buy a little time. "Is it worth it, Peg? You've already admitted to murdering two people and you seem willing to kill even more, just for Ronald Blanchard."

"Of course. He loves me." Peg's eyes blazed with a fervor that chilled Greg to the bone. "I've only done what he told me to."

"My father told you to kill Alannah? And Genie? I don't believe that," Miranda blurted out.

"Naturally. That's why he dislikes all of you girls so much. You don't listen to him and you don't obey him. And now you're causing more trouble." Peg raised the gun and Greg turned slightly to push Miranda down where she'd make less of a target. He snapped off the large flashlight as he moved, hoping that the change in light would distract Peg.

All of that angered her and whether it was reflex or intention, she fired the handgun. The sound was overpowering, reverberating off the walls of the cave. Who knew such a small gun would make that much noise and light? He spread himself over Miranda as much as possible to shield her from harm. This time he was determined to do everything he could to protect the one he loved. Old memories crowded in on him, so painful that at first he thought the burning in his shoulder was just a part of the rest of his anguish.

"Stay down," he told Miranda softly. "In a place like this any shot she fires will ricochet off the walls."

Miranda reached up toward him silently, and then gasped. "Gregory. She hit you! I feel blood."

"Good," Peg crowed. "Keep talking so I can get you, too, Miranda." She fired again and the shot zinged off a wall all too close for comfort. Even without the light from their flashlights Peg had the advantage, standing in the lit doorway. Greg couldn't understand why the light behind her seemed to flicker.

Once he did, it was too late. "You two aren't worth any more effort." Peg reached behind her and retrieved a torch. She threw it down the stairs and it splintered into several pieces. In seconds the wooden stair landing, the barrels that must have contained alcohol and the stack of tinder-dry crates blazed and crackled. Before Greg could move, Peg disappeared and slammed the door. The lock sliding home had an air of finality that mixed with her echoing laugh of triumph.

FOURTEEN

"We have to get you out of here," Miranda said, trying not to panic when she looked at Gregory. They had gone as far toward the front of the cave as possible, only to be stopped by the water obscuring the entrance. Carrying the backpack slung over his good shoulder, he was unsteady on his feet and pale. Her cotton sweater was wrapped around his upper arm and shoulder, soaked through in one spot with blood.

"How? Even if we could get past the fire Peg set, that door is locked. Nothing in my emergency pack is going to get through that. And even without this wound I'm not a strong enough swimmer to risk the undercurrent that must be pulling through the cave entrance." Greg coughed. "Maybe we can wait it out until the water recedes."

"Do you really think we can?" Miranda tried to stifle a cough herself. The acrid smoke from the burning wood made it harder to breathe with every minute.

"Honestly? I don't see how. I'm so sorry I got you into this, Miranda."

"You got me into this? The cave is under my house, and I'm the one who sat there right in front of Peg and told her where we were going. I don't see how anything in this is your fault, Gregory." She reached up and stroked his cheek, marveling at the odd sense of calm she felt. Normally situations far less harrowing than this would have her in a panic attack. Instead of panic the promise that nothing was impossible for God kept playing through her mind.

"I can't believe that God wants your life or mine to end this way." Greg sounded desperate. "It feels too familiar to me. I've been this defeated and powerless before, and everyone I loved died because of it. Now it's happening again."

"What do you mean?" Miranda kept searching for a way out, but she couldn't think of anything. She managed to lead Greg into one of the alcoves they'd seen earlier. At least here they were protected a bit from the smoke.

Greg leaned against the wall, looking exhausted. "No one in Stoneley knows my real story. A few people know that I lost my parents in an accident as a teen. What I haven't told anybody is that my whole family died in one night, and I could have stopped it from happening."

That didn't sound at all like the person she had

come to know and love. "Why are you so sure it was your fault?" Greg didn't seem to notice when Miranda eased them both down to sit on the floor of the alcove. He seemed spent, past hope.

"I should have been there. If I'd have been home instead of out with my friends, Chad wouldn't have done it. He was looking for me. He always blamed everything on me."

"Who's Chad?" It seemed so necessary to keep him talking.

"My older brother. He didn't live at home. He was sick, schizophrenic and dulling his feelings with street drugs. Part of his delusion was that I was controlling his mind. He was coming to the house to kill me, so he could be free."

"That's terrible." Hearing this, Miranda understood why Greg had been so accepting of her emotional problems: he'd seen far worse in someone he loved.

"To his disordered mind it made sense. Somehow he bought a gun and he came back to my parents' house. The police said later that he broke the lock on the back door and came in. He went to my room first and shot through the pillow on the bed, right where my head would have been. When my dad heard the shot, he came in to see what was going on. Chad just kept on shooting." His voice sounded like a stranger.

"I had blown curfew at the bowling alley with my buddies. I thought I'd sneak into the house and maybe not get caught, but when we got close to home there were police cars and lights everywhere. They wouldn't let me in the house. He shot everybody, even our little sister. She was only eleven. When he heard sirens, Chad turned the gun on himself."

Miranda's throat tightened with tears as she listened intently to his account of what had happened. Her heart ached for this compassionate man in front of her. The pain involved for him must have been nearly unbearable. "How did you go on?" She leaned forward to hear his answer. His situation sounded bleaker than the one she'd lived with, and yet here he was, strong and healthy.

"I kept asking why God let me survive. Nobody could answer that question, not in high school or college or even seminary. And now here I am at the end of my life, still asking why things happened the way they did."

Miranda felt like shaking him. If it would have done any good, she would have. "Gregory, you are not at the end of your life. And neither am I. You're the one who keeps telling me that nothing is impossible with God. There has to be a way out."

"And if there isn't?"

She took a deep breath and released it, praying for help with her answer. "Then I will be able to say I spent the end of my life with someone I loved. And after all this time, at least today I know my mother is alive."

"You're incredibly brave," Greg said, softly taking her hands in his.

"No, I'm scared silly. But thanks to you I feel God's presence in my life and with God here, I can't be overwhelmed by the spirit of fear." Miranda started coughing again.

Greg slid his pack off of his good shoulder and rummaged in it. "I don't know why I didn't think of these before." He pulled two bandannas out of the backpack. "If we wet them and tie them around the lower half of our faces, at least we'll be able to breathe better."

Miranda did what he said, and was surprised at how well it actually worked. "Now what do we do?"

"What we should have done first. We pray."

Taking Gregory's hands in hers, she set the flashlight on a ledge. He let go of her, reached over and turned it out. "We may need the batteries more later." After a moment of silence, he started. "Lord, I've never been this desperate in my life. I don't see a way out, and I've dragged this lovely young woman into the mess with me. This can't be the way You want her life to end, Father. Please, show us what to do next."

Miranda put their remaining flashlight near the first, but kept the smaller one turned on. "I want some light. It makes me feel better." Greg shrugged his shoulder and winced at the pain. She didn't like the lack of color in his face. Even in the poor light he looked ashen. "Lord, let us feel Your presence with us, no matter how things turn out. You promise never to leave us no matter what happens. Keep reminding us of that promise.

"Thank You, Lord, for bringing this incredible man into my life. And thank You for the knowledge that my mother is alive and nearby. No matter what happens to us, Father, be with her and let her make it out of this alive." Miranda's eyes filled with tears at the frustration of being so close to her mother and yet so far away. She lifted her face toward the ceiling of the cave, willing the tears not to come.

Keeping her eyes open, she felt a shock go through her. In the feeble light she could see smoke swirling around them. The gray wisps danced upward as if drawn there by some unseen force. "Gregory, let me turn on the other light."

"Sure," he said in a dull voice. Trying not to be too hopeful, Miranda added the stronger beam and aimed it toward the ceiling. In the gloom she saw something she could hardly believe.

"Gregory, you went to the Historical Society and you said they had maps. If this was a smuggler's cave, then the people who used it were probably used to being in trouble." Miranda was thinking out loud now, but he nodded. "And if they were good smugglers, they had to have another way out. A secret way."

She continued to follow the path of the smoke.

"Stop," Greg said. "Aim the light right there, and keep them both pointed up as far as possible."

"You see it, too, don't you?" The hope Miranda felt started blossoming. "There's a trapdoor up there."

"Yes, but how we are going to get that high is beyond me." Greg leaned against the wall.

Miranda looked around the cave. Back in one far corner stood two crates, rickety looking but the only thing she could see that might be of any use. Handing the lights to Greg, she went over and took hold of the crates. They actually felt sturdier than they looked. It took her precious moments to drag them into the alcove and stack them on top of one another. Praying as she went, she climbed the stack and praised God that she'd inherited her height from the Blanchards. On top of the crates she stood just feet from the ceiling of the cave. Pushing upward, she could feel something give a little. "Hand me the big flashlight, and keep praying," she told Gregory.

Using the flashlight as a tool to bang against the trapdoor, she got more and more movement at one edge. Giving the strongest push that she could, she almost fell over when the trap lifted and blessed, sweet cool air poured through.

Greg lay on the grass next to Grandma Ethel's bench, not sure he could move any farther. Getting Miranda and then himself up and through the trapdoor had used every ounce of strength he had left. It would feel so good just to lie here on the cool grass, looking up at the clouds and thanking God for their rescue. Even in his light-headed joy, he knew they couldn't do that. Peg was still in the house wreaking havoc.

"Okay. Give me a minute more and then we need to warn the others."

Miranda, sitting on the grass beside him, tilted her head. "I think it's too late for some of the warnings." When he listened he heard what she meant; somewhere a mile or two away, fire sirens wailed. Looking back at the house, dark smoke told him that Peg hadn't stopped with the fire she'd set down in the cellar entrance to the cave.

He pushed himself up to his knees, trying not to groan. Leaning on each other, they stood and went toward the house as quickly as possible. There was no way in through the back; the hallway and kitchen looked fully engulfed in flame. They went toward the front of the house as quickly as possible.

"Miranda! Greg! You're safe." Winnie hurried up to them, putting an arm around Miranda and drawing both of them away from the house and to the far edge of the circular driveway where people milled about.

"Just barely safe, Aunt. We were so wrong about everything. Peg locked us in the cave and set fire to the entrance. And she said she was going to kill Grandfather." Miranda's voice sounded ragged, and there was a smudge of soot high on her cheek.

"Peg? But I don't understand..." Winnie trailed off, looking back at the house.

Greg scanned the knots of people around them. Miranda's sisters stood together, arms around one another. Several of the servants, including Andre the chef, also stood nearby. "Where's Ronald, and the rest of the family who would have been at work?"

"On their way over. We called them from one of the cell phones just after dialing nine-one-one. They should be here soon."

The first fire trucks pulled up, the crews shouting and starting to assemble hoses and equipment while two of the firefighters went into the house, presumably to assess the situation. After a moment in the front hallway, they came back out. "Is everyone accounted for?" one of them asked.

Winnie looked around. "Not everyone. My father and his nurse have rooms on the third floor, and with the fire the elevator to the top of the house won't work." The firefighter nodded and went back to the other personnel by the truck. After conferring for a moment, two men in full gear, with oxygen tanks, went in the front door.

As Greg watched them go, he was aware of even more commotion behind him. Turning around, he saw Ronald Blanchard's car come to a screeching halt behind one of the trucks. Ronald leaped out. "Winnie. It looks worse than you told me on the phone."

"It is worse, Ronald. Peg and Father are missing."

"Oh, no. We should have moved his quarters down lower before this." As he talked Ronald ripped off his tie and tossed aside his jacket. "I've got to do something. Those firefighters can't know where Father is."

"Wait." Greg grasped the man's shoulder. "There's more to this than you think. Peg probably started this fire, and she nearly killed Miranda and me."

To his credit, Ronald didn't argue with Greg's assessment of the situation. "Then we need to get up there fast. Come on. If the front stairs can be used, we're going up."

Greg nodded, and then turned back to Miranda. "I love you. Go over there with your sisters where you'll be safe. Promise?"

Miranda looked as if she wanted to argue, but biting her lower lip a little, she merely nodded and hugged him briefly. "I promise. I'll tell them about Mama, show them the locket. Meanwhile you go with Father and tell the firefighters there are probably more people up there than we thought. But come back down quickly. You need looking after."

He marveled again at the calm she showed then. Dropping a quick but fervent kiss on her cheek, he left her in the safety of her sisters. Looking over at Ronald, Greg motioned toward the house. In a moment they were climbing the second flight of the marble stairs while he found himself telling Ronald all he knew so far about the day's strange events.

The firefighters were still going from room to

room, clearing each section, when Greg and Ronald burst into Howard's rooms. Here the smoke wasn't quite as bad yet, although the back stairs still served to suck hot air, smoke and flames up toward the top of the house.

Ronald went into the bedroom first, and Greg heard him shout "No!" He followed him in time to see Ronald pull Peg away from the bed where Howard was stretched out, a pillow in both her hands.

"But aren't you happy, dearest? I'm doing this for you. For us."

"What are you talking about?"

"You told me to do it. You said you wished someone would end his suffering. So, I'm ending it. Besides, unless he dies we can't marry."

Ronald let go of her and drew back, while Greg stood a few steps from the other two, wondering what fantasy world Peg had constructed for herself. "I have no idea what you mean. Why would I ever want to marry you?"

"Because you love me. That's so evident in everything you do. And now you love me even more because I've gotten rid of all those horrible people who were trying to ruin your life. That private investigator who threatened to bribe you, that awful woman blackmailing you, and Alannah who stood in our way. Aren't you proud of me?" The gentle seductiveness of Peg's voice and movements made Greg want to recoil.

"It's almost all done now, Ronald. Once your father is dead, I'm free to marry again."

"What on earth do you mean?" Ronald asked her as Greg looked on, as confused as Blanchard. "What does my father's death have to do with you marrying?"

"I married Howard, of course, just like you told me to," Peg said, oblivious to Ronald's noises of choked anger. "When you told me to see that his every need was met, I got him to a justice of the peace. I've done what you wanted me to all along, even when it wasn't easy. Howard was more mobile a few years ago, but he's sly. Now that sham marriage has served its purpose and I can join you, my real love, once the old fool is gone."

Greg felt shock go through him. "That's what he almost told us the other day, wasn't it? He was talking about Ethel, and then he almost told Miranda about his current wife. That's when you stopped him."

Peg turned and glared at him. "What are you doing here? How did you get out of the cave? I'm not talking to you, anyway. I'm talking to my darling Ronald." She turned back to the stunned businessman, who backed away from her.

"You're crazy," he said. "I don't know what game you're playing, but it's over now."

"No games, darling. I've only done the things you wanted me to do so that we can be together. I even made sure that Trudy won't bother you again either. It was so delicious, hiding her here in the house under her stupid daughters' noses. That was the one good idea Genie had in this whole affair."

"Trudy? Where is she?" Ronald rushed Peg, who tried to struggle out of his grasp. "Tell me what you've done with my wife."

Peg's expression changed into a grimace, and Greg almost expected her to bite Ronald as they struggled. "Nothing. That lunatic isn't your wife. Can't you see how much you need her destroyed once and for all?"

Ronald tightened his grip on the struggling woman. "The only lunatic I know about is you. And if you've harmed Trudy so close to home, I'll spend the rest of my life making sure you suffer every penalty you can. Now tell me where she is."

Greg came closer to Peg and Ronald. The man had lost all sense now, picking Peg up off the floor and shaking her like a rag doll while she hissed like a feral cat. "But what about us?" she rasped.

"Us? Get it through your head that there's no us. There's never been any 'us,'" Ronald told her, still wrestling with her even as Greg tried to break them apart. "You repulse me, you loathsome hag. I can't even believe there's any humanity left inside you. Now tell me what you did with Trudy or I'll snap your neck."

Peg went limp and Ronald lost his grip. It was the opportunity she'd been waiting for and she slid from his grasp. "You really still love her? How?" she cried. When she stood silently just out of their grasp, Greg realized that the fire was getting closer, and the smoke thicker. He could barely see across the room where Howard still lay motionless on the bed. "You can't possibly love her," Peg wailed.

"I do. I always will, and nothing you could do will change that." Ronald flung himself toward her again, but she backed away from him, her features convulsed in fear and hatred.

"You're a liar. I know you love me." She was backed into a corner now, near one of the large windows of Howard's sitting room. With a shriek she picked up a large, decorative wood-and-iron chest from the end table nearby and threw it through the window. Then, with one parting cry that reminded Greg of a wounded mountain lion, she flung herself after it.

He and Ronald rushed to the window. "No! You can't," Ronald cried. "How will we find Trudy now?"

Greg had no time to answer his question as the room filled with firefighters in masks and turnout gear.

Several people scooped Howard off the bed and, after a moment, put him on a stretcher and disappeared into the hall. Others forcibly removed Ronald and Greg from the room, dragging a protesting Ronald down the stairs and into the yard where his family surrounded him. Greg didn't fight the firefighters any. His shoulder throbbed miserably and he felt even more light-headed than he would have been just with the smoke. When they handed him over to the care of the paramedics he didn't protest.

FIFTEEN

Everything happened so quickly that Miranda didn't know how to make sense of it. Over the incredible noise of the fire there was a crash and a shriek and a form came hurtling from the third-story window. Several firefighters ran to where the body landed at the edge of the circular driveway. Mick, who had heard the call on his radio scanner and already shown up, held her and Portia back forcibly. "You are not going over there. There's nothing we can do in any case."

Before Miranda could see what was happening with the still figure on the ground, more commotion erupted at the front door of the house. Paramedics with a stretcher rushed to one of the waiting ambulances. "Grandfather," Portia gasped. "Mick, can we go over there?"

"Sure. But don't get in their way. It looks like they've started oxygen already." Portia grabbed Miranda's hand and they watched the paramedics from a few feet away.

"Is he conscious? Can we talk to him?" Miranda divided her attention between listening to the paramedic's answer and seeing if Gregory would follow the others out of the house. *Please, God,* she prayed, *keep him safe. He's so precious to me.*

"I'm afraid he's not conscious," the paramedic told Portia. "Would you have any idea what kind of medication he might have taken in the last several hours?"

"No, but his nurse..." Portia trailed off. "No, I don't know. And even if you contact his doctor from the hospital, I'm not sure everything in his system will be his prescriptions in the right amount."

"Please take care of him the best you can," Miranda said as they loaded her grandfather into the ambulance.

"Of course," the paramedic answered.

Miranda turned to look at the door and saw what she'd been hoping for. Greg and her father crossed the threshold. Greg looked more willing than her father. One of the firefighters guided Greg toward the other ambulance and a crew member helped him in. In a very short time they were examining Greg's shoulder.

"It's a deep graze," Miranda heard one of them say. "Luckily nobody's going to have to find a bullet. Start an IV and we'll get him to the E.R."

"Can I say goodbye?" Miranda asked.

At first the ambulance crew looked as if they were going to say no, but then the woman on the team, looking down at Gregory and Miranda, relented.

"Five minutes at the most. Then we toss you out of the unit and take him to the hospital," she admonished.

Miranda climbed up into the ambulance and sat down next to Greg.

"I'm okay," he said, trying to reassure her. Miranda wasn't convinced by his statement. His pale face and slight shivering didn't make him look okay to her and she told him so.

Greg tried to lift his head off the gurney but didn't have much success. "Have you seen Peg? Did she...was she..."

"She didn't make it," Miranda told him, looking over to where the firefighters covered her gently with a sheet. "Did she tell you where Mama was before she jumped?" Miranda had to assume Peg had jumped. If not, it had to have been Ronald that sent her through the window.

"No. I'm sorry, Miranda. I feel we failed you in that respect."

She brushed the hair from his forehead and kissed him gently there. "You haven't failed me in any way, Gregory. Now let them take you to the hospital and fix your shoulder. I'll be there as soon as I can."

"All right." Greg looked as if he wanted to say something more but didn't have the energy. Miranda obeyed the paramedics and got out of the ambulance, which pulled out while she made her way back to her family.

Ronald stood surrounded by his daughters and his sister, who were all talking at once. He clasped Trudy's locket in one hand and seemed to be focused on that alone.

"I can't believe she got this far and we won't be together. I'll never get to tell her how much I love her, or ask her to forgive me for all that went wrong."

Miranda had never seen her father cry before and it shocked her.

Nothing is impossible with God. The words rang in her head as clearly as if someone beside her had spoken them out loud. "We need to pray," she said firmly.

Winnie nodded, and all of them gathered even tighter and held on to each other. Miranda had one hand on her father's shoulder, and her other arm around Portia, and she could feel Juliet's arm around Portia from the other side.

"Dear Lord, help us. Help us trust in You at this dark time, and let us know that You are here with us no matter what happens. We have been searching for our mother for so long, and at every step You've reassured us that she is alive and in Your care. Now we hold this hard evidence that she's here, so close to us, Lord. Your word says that nothing is impossible for You. Please, Lord, help us do the seemingly impossible and find her before she dies in this fire."

Juliet looked up to the third-story windows

where smoke had started pouring out along one side of the house. She opened her mouth to add to the prayer but instead gave a strangled cry. "Someone's up there. Look."

They all focused to where she was pointing. "That's the attic storage room behind Father's quarters," Winnie said.

"It opens through Peg's bedroom. That has to be where they put Trudy." Ronald shook off their hands. "I'm going up there."

"No, don't. Tell the firefighters. They have the right gear," Bianca insisted. But it was too late. Ronald had already run to the house and fought his way through the doorway past the firefighters.

Bianca and Miranda went to the captain in charge and told him what was happening. He immediately got on a radio and issued orders to those in the house to apprehend Ronald and go to the third floor where they'd seen movement.

Miranda's sisters all gathered together again, praying feverishly for safety for their parents. It felt so odd to her to mention both her mother and father in the same breath with prayers for deliverance. "How long has it been?" she asked, sure that at least half an hour had gone by since Ronald had plunged into the house.

"Ten minutes," Portia said, her voice flat. Just then a knot of people came out of the house, with three firefighters surrounding Ronald.

The sight of him with a frail figure in his arms, blond hair streaming with water as he cradled the slight woman, finally made Miranda's knees give way. She sank down on the grass in tears and Bianca hugged her. "Tell me she's alive" was all she could choke out. Her sister nodded and hurried over to the spot where paramedics had taken Trudy from Ronald's arms and were administering oxygen to both of them.

The sight of people giving her mother aid made Miranda get up and follow her sisters and Winnie. She was beginning to wonder how many rescue units they had in the county to be able to call upon; two had already picked up patients bound for the hospital, and now there was a third where Trudy was being gently laid on a gurney and treated. She looked paler than the soot-smudged tan blanket someone had wrapped around her in the house, and her eyes were closed. Still, she was alive and that gave Miranda hope.

"I found her," rasped a voice behind her. Miranda turned to see her father, his dark hair singed even darker, pushing away the oxygen mask an EMT tried to put on him. "I need to talk to my daughters. Leave me alone."

"We can talk later at the hospital. Right now they need to make sure you're not badly injured. You should have let the firefighters go in there," Bianca told him, tears in her eyes.

"No time," Ronald choked out. The sound of his voice made Miranda's throat ache. "Besides…I had to tell her…so many things."

"And you did, Father." Miranda leaned down to where he sat and gave her father a genuine, loving hug. "We're so proud of you, and so thankful that you both came out of there alive."

"I'm glad. I've been a terrible father…but at least I did this…" His body shook with choking coughs and finally Ronald allowed the medics to treat him. Within minutes Miranda and her sisters were huddled together again, watching an ambulance drive away carrying both of their parents.

"We can't do anything here," Winnie said shortly. "The firefighters will save as much as they can, and it will be hours before anyone else can possibly go in there, if we go back at all today. At least at the hospital we can watch and pray where we're needed." And like a general marshalling her troops, Winnie put things in order so that half an hour later they huddled in a waiting room at Stoneley Memorial Hospital. Miranda looked around her and decided she was about to learn the real meaning of the word *vigil*.

"Are you sure you should be up and around like this?" Winnie, hands on hips, asked Gregory what Miranda wanted to ask him. He still looked pale and a bit unsteady.

"I didn't sign out against medical advice," he said, which struck Miranda as a cryptic response.

"That sounds like whoever treated you told you to go home and rest for several days, but instead here you are back at the hospital on the same day that you got shot." From the look on his face, she could tell that she'd hit the mark. "So why don't you at least sit down with us here, Gregory. I don't want to feel responsible for you passing out."

"I'm the only one who would take responsibility for that. And I wasn't shot. Even the doctors in the E.R. said it was more like a graze or a deep scratch that just happened to be caused by a bullet."

"Just happened to be caused?" Winnie's eyebrows were nearly in her hairline and Miranda knew she mirrored her aunt's reaction.

"Okay, so maybe that is a little argumentative. Besides, I wouldn't have felt right staying at home when I knew what was happening here. Even if you weren't here, your family is a part of my church and you've just lost your home and you have two family members hospitalized."

"Three," Miranda said softly. "Father found Mama, and she's alive. Greg's eyes grew wider than she'd ever seen them before.

"I believe I will take you up on that offer to sit down. How about you tell me everything that happened after I left to come here?"

It took Miranda, Winnie and Portia more than

half an hour to do just that. Somewhere in the middle of the conversation Winnie got up and made sure everyone who wanted it had a cup of tea in hand. Just about the time they came to the close of the story, Bianca arrived in the waiting room to add to the information.

"Okay, I finally got hold of Delia. She is catching the first flight possible and should be here tomorrow. Shaun is going to stay there for a few days and help her lone employee keep the shop going so that Delia won't worry as much." Miranda knew that Delia's surf shop in Hawaii was what kept her sister going. To lose it now would be devastating. She thanked God again for the wonderful men He had sent into her sisters' lives.

"Is there any more word from the fire department?" Miranda wasn't sure she wanted to know. She couldn't dwell on all that might have been lost in the fire: virtually every piece of clothing she owned, the chapbook order she'd almost finished, and much of her own poetry as well. But then, none of that mattered too much beside the fact that Trudy was alive and restored to them.

"The fire is out. It didn't consume the whole house, but a lot of the damage was to the back of the house. Peg seems to have poured gasoline or something else just as flammable up the back stairs and set a series of small fires." Bianca shuddered and Miranda went to her sister and hugged her.

"You need to sit down, too, and have Winnie get you a cup of tea. We need to stick together and be with each other through all of this."

"Always the mother hen," Bianca said, but with more generosity than usual. "You may be able to give that job up soon, you know."

The realization that her sister could be right made joy and hope warm Miranda all over again. Little bursts of those feelings had caught her by surprise for hours, ever since her father came out of the house carrying Mama in his arms. "How much longer do you think it will be before they let us in there?"

Bianca seemed to know already where "there" was for Miranda. "I asked one of the critical-care nurses on my way back here. It could still be a couple hours. After twenty-three years you'd think a few hours would be nothing." Her wry smile confirmed that those hours would be hard waiting.

By the time several doctors came to confer with Miranda and her sisters, it was after two in the morning and several family members had stretched out with blankets on the sofas and recliners in the family waiting room. Tate had come by, urging Winnie and some of the girls to go home with him and sleep in the guest rooms, but nobody was willing to leave. When he found out that Howard was on life support and had never regained consciousness, and that Ronald and Trudy were both being treated, he conceded that leaving might be a bad idea.

The doctor who briefed them was serious but not grim. "Your mother has a lot of problems. Fortunately the smoke-inhalation damage she suffered is minimal, and she has no burns. But from what I understand she's been unwillingly sedated for quite some time with a combination of drugs no doctor would prescribe together."

Rissa was the one to speak first. "Does this mean there might be brain damage?"

"We hope not. It's too soon to tell. Right now she's weak and slightly confused, but alert enough to talk to you. From what she tells me it's a meeting everyone has been waiting a long time for."

"That, Doctor, is the understatement of the year." Bianca was the one to take charge and lead everyone into the critical-care cubicle where their mother lay on the bed. Her pale hair had been washed and brushed, and the smudges of ash and soot were gone from her thin face.

"I've dreamed of this moment for so many years. It's what kept me alive in the worst of times," Trudy said, unable to check her tears. She looked at the women flanking her bed on both sides and Miranda tried to imagine what she was seeing. How did the mind handle remembering young children who now stood there as adults?

Trudy looked down at the blanket covering her, where all her daughters had unconsciously put a hand on or near her body. Then she looked up straight into Miranda's eyes. "Where's Delia? Please tell me she's alive and well. Genie and that other woman were always telling me they'd killed one of you, and I prayed they were lying to me."

Miranda felt an overpowering presence of God's spirit in the room. "They were wrong, Mama. We're all fine. Delia lives in Hawaii now and it's going to take most of a day for her to get here. But she's well, and she's married. Her husband Shaun is staying behind and watching her surf shop while she comes here."

"Okay, if nobody else is going to ask, how do you know who's who?" Juliet looked mystified.

Trudy reached out and took both of Juliet's hands in hers. "I never forgot any of you, Juliet. Children always stay in a mother's heart. Even though I haven't seen you since you were only a few months old, you're the easiest to identify. You were the only one who had my green eyes." Trudy swallowed hard. "There's something I need to confess to you about that."

"I know, Mom. And so does everybody else."

"I'm sorry for the pain that must have caused you. I can't imagine that Ronald was kind about it." She closed her eyes for long enough that Miranda wondered if she'd gone to sleep.

"We should let you rest. We'll be outside when you feel like talking again."

Trudy smiled. "That will be wonderful." She

closed her eyes again and her daughters left the room. Miranda could tell that her sisters were as reluctant to leave as she was.

"We need to see how Father and Grandfather are doing," Miranda said. "Maybe Gregory can get more information than we could. I imagine he's at the hospital often to visit people. He must have connections."

When they got back to the family room, Miranda went to talk to Gregory only to find him sound asleep leaning back on one of the cushions of a bench. After everything he'd been through, she couldn't wake him.

Bianca, who had assumed her attorney role and taken charge since they arrived at the hospital, was the one to find the right doctors. "I know that my grandfather has a living will. But it may be a while before we can produce a copy. Between the fire and our father being incapacitated as well…"

"That's a more pressing subject," the doctor told them. "I'm the pulmonary specialist for both your father and grandfather, and of the two I'd say you have more to worry about with your father. The smoke damage to his lungs is severe. The next twenty-four hours will decide whether he lives or not."

The shock radiating through the room felt like a living thing. "We need to be informed every hour, then," Bianca told him. The others voiced a muffled chorus of agreement.

"Even more often if necessary. We'll do all we can, and he seems to be a fighter."

"You have no idea," Miranda said, thankful for the first time in her life for her father's stubborn disposition.

By daybreak it was apparent that it was only his strong constitution and stubborn streak keeping Ronald alive. "I need Trudy," he wrote on the pad he had insisted be brought to him. Having a way to write was the only reason he agreed to the breathing tube the doctors insisted he needed. Even then he wouldn't agree to the pain medications they wanted him to have, or to be transferred to a larger hospital where they had even more advanced treatment. "Too much to do," he wrote and underlined.

This was such a different man from the one Miranda was used to seeing. It pained her that she might only get to know him for a day or two. After reading his request for her mother, Miranda decided it was time to wake Greg and ask his help in dealing with this situation. He looked startled for a moment. "How long have I been asleep?"

"Over three hours. I couldn't stand to wake you."

He smiled at her. "You're too kind. If you needed me, you shouldn't have let me sleep this long."

"I let you sleep until I really needed you, Gregory. I think we're at a point where you need to get involved." She told him about her father's medical status, and his request to have Trudy brought to his bedside. "I want somebody else with me when I ask her what she wants to do."

Greg took a deep breath, looking thoughtful. "Okay. I can do that. Are you prepared to accept your mother's answer no matter which way it goes?"

"Definitely. But if she refuses to see him, I'm going to need help going back to Father to tell him that."

Miranda had a hard time reading Greg's expression. "I don't think that's going to be a problem," he told her.

After their journey of the last twenty-four hours together, she wasn't about to argue with him. And even though Miranda had her reservations, her mother didn't seem to have any. When Greg broke the news to her that Ronald might not live more than another day or two, she insisted on going to him. So after prayer and discussion with Gregory, and a bit of a fight with the nursing staff, Trudy was wheeled into Ronald's ICU cubicle. Miranda sat in the waiting room outside the ICU with Greg, gripping his hand and praying for her parents.

SIXTEEN

It was only ten in the morning and Greg felt it had to be seven or eight in the evening again. He hadn't had a day filled with this kind of emotional upheaval in twenty years. Through everything, he marveled at Miranda and her quiet courage. For someone who only weeks before was chained to her home by panic attacks, she had made incredible progress. He continued to be moved by the examples of God's grace in her life and in the lives of her family.

While he sat with her outside the ICU where her parents worked out issues he could only imagine, Winnie found them. Her face was puffy and tear streaked. "Pastor Greg, I hate to ask you for even more help, but you're the only one I can imagine helping me."

"Is it something regarding your father?" Greg wondered how possibly losing her father and brother within days of each other might affect this woman. For anyone of lesser faith he would have worried about their spiritual well-being. With Winnie he worried more about what kind of physical toll the loss would take on a woman of sixty, even one as healthy as Miranda's aunt.

"Yes, it's Father. He is still unresponsive and his doctors are afraid that he may never regain consciousness. And on top of everything else he's showing signs of pneumonia." Winnie's shoulders slumped. "After all he's been through lately, I had hoped he'd go quietly in his own bed. Now it doesn't seem that's going to happen."

"Shall we find the hospital chapel, or do you want me to go with you to sit at his bedside?"

"I think perhaps the chapel," Winnie said. "I need to feel some peace to discover God's will in all of this."

Nodding, Greg looked at Miranda. "Do you want to go with us or wait here? I can make sure on our way to the chapel that some of your sisters come join you."

"I'll go get them. You be with Winnie." Miranda stood and gave her aunt a gentle hug. "This just isn't what we expected, is it?"

"Not the best or the worst of it. I kept hoping we'd find Trudy alive and well. I never dreamed she'd turn up under our roof."

The three of them walked as far as the waiting room, where the rest of the Blanchards gathered. Then Miranda joined her sisters and Greg guided Winnie to the small hospital chapel. He felt thankful that they had the place to themselves. With all the serious cases that came through Stoneley Memorial, there was often more than one family here seeking comfort or guidance.

They weren't alone there for long. Before Greg could do much more than start praying aloud for guidance, a doctor rushed into the room. "Miss Blanchard, you need to come with me now. And if this is your pastor, you may want him to join us."

A quick trip through the halls and on an elevator marked Staff Only brought them to Howard's bedside. "His heart rhythm is irregular and I understand he doesn't wish to be resuscitated."

"That's correct. Is he in any pain?" Winnie's face looked drawn.

"No. He's nearly comatose and beyond any pain he might have felt earlier." In a few moments Miranda and her sisters slipped into the room by ones and twos. When Greg started reciting the Twenty-third Psalm he could hear Winnie and several of her nieces join him. With those sweet, low voices surrounding him, Howard Blanchard slipped out of this life.

"Should we tell Father?" Miranda asked when it was over.

"If I were making the decision, I might wait for him to ask. He'll probably know without being told." Greg couldn't find the words to explain to her why this was so, but he'd seen it more than once in the past seven years.

"Even if you don't tell him right away, you need to go to him," Winnie told him. "And you girls need to go as well. Leave me here with your grandfather a while. And if someone would call Tate I'd appreciate it."

Bianca gave a tremulous smile. "I already did that, Aunt Winnie. He should be here anytime."

"Then let's go back to the ICU," Greg said. "I want to be there when your parents finish talking."

"Me, too," Miranda said, taking his hand.

"We're going to break the rules," Ronald's nurse told them when they got to the ICU. "You're going to help me and you're going to keep quiet about it, right?"

"Right." Greg knew this particular nurse and if she was asking him to break a hospital rule, it had to be important.

"There should only be two people in with Mr. Blanchard at the same time, but I think the four of you need to be in there together."

He didn't argue. When they got into the cubicle the sight that met them surprised him. Ronald and Trudy were holding hands and Trudy was insisting that Ronald put his oxygen mask back on. "I promise, Ron, I'll tell them exactly what you said. You can listen and if I don't, you can take that thing off, all right?

"You're the pastor at Unity, aren't you? Ron wants you to marry us, and do it within the next half hour, because he says he's ready to die. I'd believe he didn't have a chance, expect that I've heard from his nurses that if he'd agree to be transferred to another hospital they could save him." She looked over at Ronald. "Is that right so far?"

Ronald nodded, still looking as if he wanted to take off the mask. "I've told Ron that we both need to work some things out, to confess things to each other and to God before we consider remarrying. I've also told him that I'll promise to marry him again if he goes to Portland to the…the…what do they call it?" She looked over at Ronald again and he wrote on his notepad.

"Right. The hyperbaric chamber. Will you witness that promise, Reverend Brown? And would you agree to marry us if he fulfills his part of it?"

Normally a decision like this was something Greg would approach with a couple of days of reading Scripture, prayer and talking at length to everybody involved. This time these two people needed him to make a decision in twenty minutes or less.

"I think I've already witnessed the promise by listening to you, Trudy. And I'll agree to perform a marriage ceremony if you're both sure you want it."

"All right. Now will you get on the helicopter, Ron?"

Ronald grimaced and pulled aside the mask for a moment. "If I want to marry you, do I have a choice?"

"Put that back on. And no, you don't."

Greg looked over at Miranda, who had watched all this silently. Tears trickled down her cheeks. "Now how are we going to get the rest of us to Portland if you go by helicopter, Father?"

Ronald ripped off the top page of paper on his notepad. "Private plane. Take everybody that will fit with your mother," he wrote.

While the rest of what he'd seen from Ronald Blanchard today had been different, this looked like the old take-charge Ronald. Normally he'd be dismayed by that but right now it felt like another gift from God.

He turned to share that feeling with Miranda but she was gone, beside her mother and talking about getting to the hospital. "You're here with us, Mama, and that's all that matters. We'll work it all out no matter what it takes." They didn't notice when Greg left the cubicle.

Was this the last time she would see Gregory? Miranda looked up to where the handsome pastor stood in the pulpit delivering the eulogy at her grandfather's funeral.

Unity was filled with people. After six years of his illness, Miranda was amazed that this many people would mourn the passing of Howard Blanchard. At least the hordes of tabloid reporters had come and gone now, perhaps for the last time. When the family had presented a solid front after the fire that nearly destroyed their home, the media had focused on Peg Henderson instead. In her life and history they'd found plenty of fodder for numerous scandalous stories.

How had Peg ever hidden her past so thoroughly when she'd targeted Howard as her next victim? Miranda couldn't imagine living an entire life with as much lying, deceit and scheming as Peg had in forty-five years. Her burial had been attended only by a few reporters who noted that the Blanchard family made sure she wasn't buried in an unmarked grave. Now, several days later, those same reporters sat in some of the back rows of Howard's memorial.

The front row of the church filled Miranda with a sense of awe. Only a week after the fire her parents sat together clasping hands. Trudy had a complex plan of therapy to follow that took her back to the hospital on a daily basis. And Ronald in his dark suit didn't show the trauma of late. He was only here for the service, with six women prepared to escort him back to his room at Stoneley Memorial if he showed the least sign of flagging. In fact there were probably more like eight women, if his assistant Barbara Sanchez and his sister were added to the mix. Both had clucked over him almost as much as Trudy and his daughters.

Life might have been perfect except for one thing: the last time she'd had a moment alone with Gregory was when they walked to the intensive care unit after her grandfather's death. And the lack of communication seemed to suit him just fine. It was as if he'd come to a decision that the two of them were, after all, just friends. The sadness Miranda felt over that was deeper than the loss of her grandfather. At least she had the comfort that Howard was done with his pain and confusion, and she could picture him reunited with Grandmother Ethel.

Gregory motioned Ronald up to the pulpit to speak. Miranda and her sisters had argued against it, but their father insisted. His voice was still raspy and low from the smoke damage, and he had to lean closer to the microphone than he normally would. She had never noticed how much silver streaked his temples these days, or perhaps the past two weeks had painted more there.

"My father, Howard Blanchard, was a proud and self-reliant man. Before illness dimmed his senses, he was known as one of the sharpest businessmen in New England. He groomed me to follow in his footsteps and, God help me, for many years I did just that. To quote Charles Dickens, we both should have realized that 'mankind should have been our business,' not striving to make a bigger company out of Blanchard Fabrics.

"To his credit, I will say that my father loved his granddaughters fiercely. They were his joy even after Alzheimer's disease made it difficult for him to recognize them on occasion. When I was a child he showed me and my sister the same kind of love. It was only after we lost my mother that he became quite as intense about his work. When my mother died it was as if the light of his life went with her. I can only hope now that he has found God's peace."

Ronald stood silently and collected himself for a moment, and took a swallow of the water that Greg had placed there for him. He seemed to sway slightly, and Miranda almost got out of her seat. She noticed that her mother, Bianca and Winnie all seemed to mirror her action. They all visibly relaxed when he straightened and went on.

"I was not able to be at my father's bedside for his passing, but Pastor Greg has told me that the family members who were there recited the Twenty-third Psalm as he died. I know that hearing that passage was a comfort to him in his last years of life and I regret that I didn't think to read it to him far more often than I did. As a tribute to him and as a testimony to the Lord I know he believed in, I'd like to ask you to recite it with me now."

The crowd had joined him by the time Ronald got to "I shall not want," and Miranda felt lifted up by hearing the words of comfort on so many lips.

When her father went back to his seat, Gregory spoke about Howard's last days and the unfortunate nature of his death. He didn't go into detail but merely noted that the family had done everything in their power to make sure he was comfortable and in familiar surroundings as long as possible. "It's a shame that intent was taken away from them by someone they trusted. The doctors have tried to assure the family that Howard was unaware of the trauma to the home he cared for so deeply. They tell us he slipped away peacefully to another mansion, one that was prepared for him long ago."

At the end of the service Gregory announced to those present that after a short graveside service everyone was welcome to join the family back at Unity's fellowship hall. In any other circumstance Miranda knew that everyone would have gone back to the house, but there was no house to go back to. For now they were taking up half-a-dozen rooms at the inn while Tate Connolly, Brandon and Leo all scrambled to set up temporary living quarters in properties they owned near town.

The next few hours blurred together. Miranda never lost sight of Gregory but at the same time never made eye contact, either. She went back and forth to the cemetery in the same limousine as Delia, Bianca and Leo, none of them saying much. Back at the church she made tepid conversation with people she barely knew who expressed their sympathy for her loss when she really felt like asking them how they could possibly understand what she had lost.

There was a knot in her throat and she had to get out of this building. Picking up her cup of tea,

Miranda went outside to the gardens surrounding the church. They'd anticipated so many people coming to her grandfather's services that someone had erected several green-and-white striped pavilions. It was only after she sat down at a table under one that it reminded her of the wedding reception where she'd first met Greg. It was less than a month ago, but felt like a lifetime.

A month ago she would have collapsed in a panic attack in a situation like this, but that was all in the past. Instead Miranda just buried her face in her hands and gave in to the tears that threatened to swamp her.

"I can't do this anymore." The deep voice sounded in her ear just before Gregory pulled her up out of her chair, wrapping his arms around her. "I know half of Stoneley is watching and I know you don't love me but I can't watch you cry."

She pulled the crisp linen handkerchief out of the breast pocket of his suit, unwilling to move otherwise for fear he'd let go of her. "Of course I love you, Gregory. What could make you think otherwise?"

"You didn't need me anymore after you found your mother, and I didn't want to force myself on you. You've lost so much, Miranda, and through it all I watched you grow in faith and confidence. When you told your mother that day at the hospital that her well-being was all that mattered I knew it was time to let you go."

"Gregory, the only loss I've had in the last ten

days that really mattered was thinking I'd lost your love. After you told me about your family down in the cave, you seemed to shut down. Then Peg shot you and she could have killed you all on my account." Her voice shook. "How could I possibly ask you to be with me after that? I'm the imperfect product of an extremely imperfect family and I may never get any better than I am right now."

He tilted her head up to face him and just the feel of his fingertips under her chin made a thrill go through her.

"Would it help to know I don't care? That I think you're the most courageous person I've ever met, and I'd like to see how that courage ages for at least the next fifty or sixty years?" Greg said.

"Sixty years?" Miranda wanted to giggle. "That would make us both over ninety, Gregory."

"Hey, you're the one who keeps reminding me that for God, nothing is impossible. I told you that once, Miranda, and you've brought it back into my life so that I believe it in a whole new way."

Miranda could see the promise of his love through her tears. "So do I. It won't ever get old, will it, this knowing that for God anything is possible? Even working something out for people like the two of us?"

"Especially for working life out for people like us, love. And not just people like us, but for us particularly. It's His promise to us."

Smiling up at Greg, Miranda felt no surprise at all when he sealed his words with a kiss.

"Good," she told him when he let her breathe again. "I want to see what impossibility He gets us through first."

EPILOGUE

Fourteen months later

"Winnie, you throw the best parties. You should charge for these services." Greg dropped a kiss on the top of her head as she sat at the table set up in the rose garden.

Miranda loved watching her husband interact with her family. They got together much less frequently these days, but this weekend held so many events she'd seen her parents and sisters nonstop.

"Nonsense, Greg. It wouldn't be any fun if I did it for any reason but sheer pleasure. And believe me, this anniversary party is sheer pleasure." Winnie beamed, reaching next to her for Tate's hand and giving it a squeeze. He smiled back and Miranda thought once again how wonderful it had been to watch her aunt and the man she now called Uncle Tate grow into the loving married couple she saw now.

Even more amazing was the couple on the other side of the table. Ronald and Trudy Blanchard still had their moments, but the relationship God had built from the ashes of their former lives was a true miracle.

"What about tomorrow's dedication? Will that be pure pleasure, too?" Miranda sat down in the empty chair on the other side of Winnie, where she could see her aunt and still keep her eye on Greg's reaction.

"It's pleasant in an entirely different way," Winnie said, still smiling. "This place needed a new life and I'm so happy to be a part of making it come about."

"I'm just glad to see it stop taking up your time," Tate harrumphed. "How am I supposed to teach you the finer points of golf when you're always party planning?"

Winnie shook her head. "You know I don't spend any more hours on my volunteer work than you do 'consulting' for the company."

"All right, no sniping. You'll start sounding like us," Ronald said, wagging a finger at his sister.

"Ron, honestly. The girls will think you mean that," Trudy chided gently.

"They'll think nothing of the kind," Ronald said jovially. This openness was a side of her father Miranda never got tired of. "They are all too busy sighing over their own husbands and thinking dreamily of their first anniversaries to come, like ours and the Connellys', to worry about what I'm saying."

"Hey, I heard that!" Delia, who cruised by the

table with an icy fruit drink in hand that almost matched her flowing Hawaiian sundress, put her free hand on her father's shoulder. "And I'll have you know I'm not thinking about anniversaries at all. I'm trying to figure out how I sweet-talk you into lending me Mom alone for about a month to help set up the nursery and look after me and this new grandbaby when it's time." She sighed dreamily. "Shaun has already put together the most beautiful bassinet, and now I want to decorate the room around it."

"You might have to put up with both of us. I don't know if I can let her out of my sight that long," Ronald said, his eyes only on Trudy.

"That would mean you'd have to let somebody else run Seasons while you're gone. Do you think you could stand that?" Trudy was forever testing his devotion to the reformed fabric company that now bore part of its original name again.

"For you, my dear, I'd walk away from it permanently. You know that," Ronald told her.

Hearing that proclamation made Miranda's heart swell in amazement at what God had worked in her father.

"Hawaii? Did I hear somebody's going to Hawaii?" Kaitlyn Campbell raced up to the table, all seven-year-old high spirits. "Mom and Dad said next time we would all go, but we'd have to wait until after the baby's born." Portia and Mick, gathered with a few others from Unity, seemed to know their daughter was talking about them. From across the garden Portia waved, her other arm around her husband's waist.

Delia leaned down to embrace her niece. "You can come whenever your parents say it's all right, kiddo. Maybe they'd let me borrow you for Christmas break and we could start putting you on a boogie board."

Miranda thought about telling Delia that she might not feel up to that only a few weeks after giving birth, but she kept silent. Her sisters were all grown women, happily married with lives of their own. Besides, they had a mother to point out such things. Her job as the oldest sister was just to watch it all happen and enjoy it now.

"You've got to be careful what you say around here," Juliet broke in. "Next thing you know, the word's going to go around that Delia and Shaun are having us all come for a Christmas party. Do you think you'd be ready for a baby dedication by then, too? We could get there from Paris, couldn't we, Brandon?"

"Probably, if the design house lets you off and I could figure out some way to let somebody else run the European branch of Seasons, International, for a week or so," her handsome husband said. "But that would mean celebrating our first anniversary in Hawaii with the family. Are you up for that?"

"Always," Juliet said with a grin. "If this keeps up, we're going to need to find some kind of bed-and-breakfast inn on Oahu to accommodate everybody."

"And who's paying for this? New York City police officers don't make the kind of bucks corporate lawyers and business tycoons do," Drew said. Rissa's husband looked stern for a moment and Brandon began to apologize. Then Drew couldn't hold his expression any longer and laughed. "Don't worry about it, man. Rissa's play will open off-Broadway by then and I think we can manage. It's just fun to annoy you."

"Who's annoying who over here?" Bianca joined the group. "Somebody who isn't being annoying can help me find Leo. I think he's slipped off somewhere to make a few business calls on his cell phone and I want help reminding my husband that we agreed this was a 'family only' weekend."

"Surely you can find some creative way to do it yourself," Trudy suggested, bringing a slight blush to her daughter's cheeks.

"Back to the dedication tomorrow," Winnie said, her attitude more businesslike. "How much time should we allow for your talk, Greg?"

Miranda could see her husband pale for a moment, and then straighten up. "Not long. Only about ten minutes at the most. I figured that you and Ronald would be doing most of the talking. After all, it's your parents that this place will honor."

Miranda looked across the lawn to where the newly finished Howard and Ethel Blanchard Memorial Clinic stood ready to open its doors. The sprawling brick building was a far cry from the mansion her family had left after the fire. No one wanted to live there anymore after Peg's destruction of the place.

"It has our name on it, son, but you better get used to talking about it. The director of New England's largest Christian counseling center will need to have a voice," Ronald told Greg.

"I suppose you're right, sir. I'm still getting used to that, especially since I only consider myself the acting director until I finish school. That's going to take years."

"You've got such a gift for counseling, Gregory," Trudy put in. "I can't imagine finishing a doctorate in psychology will be overwhelming, especially at such a fine Christian school."

Greg shrugged. "I'll need the family prayer chain surrounding me for a while. I know that God has His hand on this undertaking, but it still overwhelms me at times."

"This family can always surround us with prayer," Miranda said, getting up and putting an arm around her husband. "They're very, very good at it now that they've come back together with God as the head of the clan."

"Amen," Gregory told her, sealing the statement

with a kiss. There in the garden, life continued with
a celebration around them and Miranda knew, no
matter what happened next, that with God's love and
her family's help, life would unfold as He intended.

* * * * *

Dear Reader,

I hope you've enjoyed THE SECRETS OF STONELEY series of books that we've brought to you over the past six months. What I enjoy the most about a set of books like this is the sisterhood that builds between the authors as they write the books. Like Miranda and her sisters, we share joys and sorrows with each other, serve as prayer partners during the challenges of writing and just generally support each other. I hope the ups and downs of the Blanchard sisters will motivate you to call or e-mail or visit a sister—or a sister in Christ— and share the Good News with her.

Blessings,

Lynn Bulock

QUESTIONS FOR DISCUSSION

1. The theme verse for this book reminds us that nothing is impossible for God. What seemingly impossible things has God done in your life, or the life of someone you know?

2. The Blanchard family kept secrets from each other for generations, leading to a fractured family relationship for everyone. Do you think it's ever all right to keep these kinds of secrets within a family? Why or why not?

3. How did the family handle Ronald's arrest? What would you have done in their place?

4. Did the Blanchard family end up the way you thought they would? What would you change if you were writing their story?

5. Miranda spent most of her life letting anxiety rule over her. If you had a friend like Miranda, what would you tell her?

6. How did Howard Blanchard's battle with Alzheimer's disease affect his family? Do you think they made the right choices in caring for him?

7. When Miranda needed help outside her family, she had a support group to turn to. Who is your support group, and what do they help you with the most?

8. What support could Winnie give Miranda as a relative? In what way can relatives sometimes find it difficult to help loved ones? Why do you think that is? What can we do to change that?

9. What might have been different for the Blanchard family if their views on mental or emotional illness had been less rigid?

10. What surprised you the most about the person responsible for the murders? Do you think it's possible to conceal a character as flawed as this person's?

Love Inspired®

Celebrate Love Inspired's 10th anniversary with top authors and great stories all year long!

FOR HER SON'S LOVE

BY KATHRYN SPRINGER

A Tiny Blessings Tale

Loving families and needy children continue to come together to fulfill God's greatest plans!

With the legality of her son's adoption in question, Miranda Jones knows she can't trust anyone in Chestnut Grove with her secrets—especially Andrew Noble. He was working his way into her heart, but his investigation into her past could tear her family apart.

Available July wherever you buy books.

Steeple Hill®

LIFHSL

REQUEST YOUR FREE BOOKS!
2 FREE RIVETING INSPIRATIONAL NOVELS
PLUS 2 FREE MYSTERY GIFTS

Love Inspired®
SUSPENSE

YES! Please send me 2 FREE Love Inspired® Suspense novels and my 2 FREE mystery gifts. After receiving them, if I don't wish to receive any more books, I can return the shipping statement marked "cancel." If I don't cancel, I will receive 4 brand-new novels every month and be billed just $3.99 per book in the U.S. or $4.74 per book in Canada, plus 25¢ shipping and handling per book and applicable taxes, if any*. That's a savings of 20% off the cover price! I understand that accepting the 2 free books and gifts places me under no obligation to buy anything. I can always return a shipment and cancel at any time. Even if I never buy another book from Steeple Hill, the two free books and gifts are mine to keep forever.

123 IDN EL5H   323 IDN ELQH

Name	(PLEASE PRINT)	
Address		Apt. #
City	State/Prov.	Zip/Postal Code

Signature (if under 18, a parent or guardian must sign)

Order online at www.LoveInspiredSuspense.com

Or mail to Steeple Hill Reader Service™:

IN U.S.A.: P.O. Box 1867, Buffalo, NY 14240-1867
IN CANADA: P.O. Box 609, Fort Erie, Ontario L2A 5X3

Not valid to current Love Inspired Suspense subscribers.

Want to try two free books from another series?
Call 1-800-873-8635 or visit www.morefreebooks.com

* Terms and prices subject to change without notice. NY residents add applicable sales tax. Canadian residents will be charged applicable provincial taxes and GST. This offer is limited to one order per household. All orders subject to approval. Credit or debit balances in a customer's account(s) may be offset by any other outstanding balance owed by or to the customer. Please allow 4 to 6 weeks for delivery.

Your Privacy: Steeple Hill is committed to protecting your privacy. Our Privacy Policy is available online at www.eHarlequin.com or upon request from the Reader Service. From time to time we make our lists of customers available to reputable firms who may have a product or service of interest to you. If you would prefer we not share your name and address, please check here. ☐

LISUS07

Love Inspired SUSPENSE

TITLES AVAILABLE NEXT MONTH

Don't miss these four stories in July

NO LOVE LOST by Lynn Bulock
Cozy mystery

She married a murderer? Gracie Lee Harris was sure Hal, her ex-husband, didn't have *that* dark a side. But with her ex as the prime suspect in his fiancée's death and her boyfriend, Ray Fernandez, as the lead investigator, Gracie could only pray that Hal's secrets wouldn't get *her* killed!

DEATH BENEFITS by Hannah Alexander
A HIDEAWAY novel

Attending a wedding in Hawaii seemed the perfect tropical dream to Ginger Carpenter...until an escaped convict began stalking her young foster nieces. To protect them, she would have to rely on Dr. Ray Clyde—the one man she never wanted to see again.

VALLEY OF SHADOWS by Shirlee McCoy
A LAKEVIEW novel

Heartbroken following the death of her nephew, the last thing Miranda Shelton expected was to become involved in a DEA investigation. Yet now she and Agent Hawke Morran were running for their lives, desperate to uncover the truth behind the betrayal that brought them together.

DANGEROUS SECRETS by Lyn Cote
Harbor Intrigue

The town of Winfield's peacefulness was shattered by the bizarre death of Sylvie Patterson's cousin. And as the last person to see him alive, Sylvie was square in the sights of investigator Ridge Matthews. But as another family member died and Ridge got closer to the truth, they must learn to trust in each other—and God—to uncover the deadly secrets lurking in her once quiet town.

LISCNM0607